THE CELTIC BOOK
OF SEASONAL MEDITATIONS

THE CELTIC BOOK
OF SEASONAL
MEDITATIONS

CLAIRE HAMILTON

With a foreword by Marian Green

Red Wheel
Boston, MA / York Beach, ME

First published in 2003 by
Red Wheel/Weiser, LLC
P. O. Box 612
York Beach, ME 03910-0612
www.redwheelweiser.com

Library of Congress Cataloging-in-Publication Data available upon request.
ISBN 1-59003-055-9

Typeset in Sabon

PRINTED IN THE UNITED STATES OF AMERICA
RRD

08 07 06 05 04 03
8 7 6 5 4 3 2 1

The paper used in this publication meets the minimum requirements of the American
National Standard for Information Sciences—Permanence of Paper for Printed Library
Materials Z39.48-1992 (R1997).

CONTENTS

VERY LAND has its legendary heritage, a collection of tales, poetry and song, which, though eroded through time, rewritten and altered in the retelling has survived for hundreds of years. In the misty British Isles and Western Europe one strand of this magical thread is that of the Celts, who have passed down to us a treasure of hero tales, myths of ancient gods and goddesses and legends of kings and queens. This wonderful collection of philosophy, poetry and visionary material, which in the twentieth and twenty-first centuries is reaching a new and wider audience, is inspiring again the works of songsters, bards and people who draw on its magic and pagan roots in their beliefs and work.

Because the original peoples, called Keltoi by the Greeks, have not left us their names, nor did they write down the titles of the gods, or the content of their

Foreword
by Marian Green

stories, modern commentators have had to rebuild much of their works. It is widely accepted that the Celtic peoples had a cycle of annual festivals based upon the gifts of the land as the seasons passed, and the animals brought forth young, or milk, or meat and hides, and these are being celebrated again. We cannot know for certain how the old feasts were marked, but if we examine the vast store of tales we can begin to find patterns. There are the many questing stories, where the young hero has to find his name, or his weapons or his inheritance, and the legends of voyages when a treasure is sought. Both of these echo older Greek tales, when the hero and his companions set out, against the odds, to bring back the Golden Fleece or overcome some monster. Where the Greeks sought the riches of gold, the Celtic heroes quested for the Cauldron from the Otherworld which would restore life.

Many of today's seekers have done as I did: re-read the old stories and seen that though the setting may be the castles of the West, or the mystical regions of the Otherworld, there are clues which anyone can follow into the turmoil and concrete jungles of the modern world. We still need to discover our true name and learn what task we are destined to complete and what taboos we must avoid. We can rediscover the wisdom of Ceridwen's Cauldron, or the underlying support of the Stone of Destiny, if we are ready to venture beyond the confines of this frantic world into the silence of past realms. If we enter the stillness of a meditation, walk the wandering mindways of the ancient peoples, recognise their sacred places and times, we can draw strength and calmness from the mystical regions.

The guidance for readers given here will steer anyone through the labyrinth of tales, introduce the heroes and heroines of the Celts, explain their stories and reveal the bounty for soul and body hidden there. It does take patience and commitment but these are a small fee for such ancient wisdom and internal awakening as such material can provide. Tread again the old byways of the land, in reality or in mind, seek out the gifts of the old ones, and be enriched by this heritage.

MARIAN GREEN, Somerset, March 2002

A T A TIME when age-old certainties are being questioned and other values sought, it is challenging and refreshing to look back to an ancient society that had a radically different outlook on life. The name Celt comes from the Greek *Keltoi*, meaning "The Mysterious Ones." The Greeks gave them this name because they considered them a strange and mysterious people, as did the Romans. This was because the Celtic attitude to life was alien to theirs in at least three fundamental areas. They were a matriarchal society, they had a great reverence for the earth, and they believed in the close proximity of the spirit world.

Today there are those who consider that Celtic understanding offers a valuable corrective to the perils of modern society. Their matriarchal values are attractive to us at a time when patriarchal values are being questioned and overturned; their reverence for nature beckons to us at a time when natural

Introduction

resources are coming under threat; and in an age where science has been given the upper hand, their visionary and spiritual way of life offers us new ways of perceiving the world.

Much of Celtic spiritual understanding came from their living close to nature. They believed that the earth contained numerous gateways to the Otherworld, the world of spirit. Their shamans and holy men were highly respected, and received long years of training, enabling them to shapechange into the form of animals, or even into the elements themselves, and to experience different and illuminating levels of existence. The wisdom that they received from these experiences enabled them to offer a different perspective on life. From their spiritual journeyings they brought back knowledge of the mysterious, the numinous, the occult. We might say today that they placed a great value on intuition, which balances out the rational view of life.

It has been argued that because we know so little about the Celts, it is easy to create a magical fantasy around them and to turn the Dark Ages into a misty "golden age." This is of course a temptation, especially because the Celts considered the word so sacred that in their society it was forbidden to write anything down, which means that they cannot speak to us directly from their time. However, they can and do speak to us in other ways. They speak through their art, their artefacts, their burial sites, their altars and symbolic inscriptions, and their myths. It is from all these, therefore, that our picture of them has been constructed.

Much of our archaeological evidence concerning the Celts was discovered in the nineteenth century. In 1846 a prehistoric cemetery was uncovered at Hallstatt near Salzburg in Austria. This was an early site dated to between 700 and 500 BCE and contains some two and a half thousand graves. The artefacts that have come to light are made of iron and include horse-harnesses, pots, vessels, chariots and swords, some of which are decorated with gold-leaf, ivory and amber. The next and more sophisticated phase of Celtic civilisation comes from the site of La Tène in Switzerland discovered in 1858. The finds here date from 500 BCE and include cups and wine vessels, bronze flagons, weapons and jewellery. The decoration on these artefacts is much more refined and there is extensive use of the characteristic Celtic flowing patterns.

From such discoveries it has been deduced that the Celtic people extended at one time from Ireland and part of Spain across to Hungary and Czechoslovakia, and from Scotland down to the top of Italy. Even though they were not so much a people as a body of linked tribes, they stood out from other races at that time, being strongly united by their religious beliefs and customs.

Although the Celts wrote nothing down themselves, we can glimpse their beliefs and the ordering of their society through Greek and Roman writers. From Strabo, for example, we learn about the Druids. He tells us they were divided into three main categories, the Bard, Ovate and Druid. Caesar tells us that the Druids were not just the priests of the people, they were also their judges and advisors to their kings. He also reports that they studied all branches of the sciences and contemplated moral philosophy. Polybius tells us about the character of the Celts, saying that they are headstrong and passionate. As regards appearance, Diodorus says that they bleached their hair in lime-water and wore it tied back like a horse's mane, whereas Herodian asserts that they disliked wearing clothes and adorned themselves with ornaments and tattooed patterns instead.

The Celts were extremely brave in war as numerous other accounts testify. They went out to battle inspired by emotional heroism and the magical invocation of the Druids. To the disciplined Roman armies they seemed barbaric in the extreme. It is evident that the so-called "civilised" peoples such as the Greeks and Romans, who used the written word without a qualm, considered these people who had a way of life they were unable to understand, and who refused to record their knowledge in written records, naïve and primitive. Even though such writers were often critical and prejudiced in their observations, their comments are extremely illuminating.

But the great body of writing that most informs the Celtic scholar are the myths. These were recorded by the Christian monks. They were the overthrowers of the ancient Druidic wisdom on which Celtic society depended, yet they were also the recorders of such wisdom. For, even though they tried to overlay the old tales with Christianity, much of the ancient understanding still shines through.

The body of Irish myths is extensive. There are three main cycles: the Mythological Cycle, the Ulster Cycle and the Fionn Cycle. The Mythological cycle includes the Book of Invasions. This gives an account of several waves of peoples who apparently conquered Ireland during very early times. Most famous of these were the *Tuatha de Danann*, who conquered the two giant races, the Firbolgs and the Fomorians. The Tuatha were conquered in their turn by the Milesians, who made a curious treaty with them. The Tuatha were allowed to remain, provided they retreated into the earth and lived in the burial mounds and tumuli. These were thereafter known as the *sidhe*, or faerie mounds, for the Tuatha became the faerie people. As such they could be alluring and dangerous, for they could entice mortals to the Land of Youth, a magical Otherworld. Many stories concern such journeys, which are at times a benefit and at others a snare.

The Ulster Cycle concerns the exploits of the hero Cuchulainn and the Red Branch Warriors. It includes the tragic tale of Deirdre, who was fated to fall in love with Naoise and thereby bring ruin to Ulster. It also includes the famous tale of the Cattle Raid of Cooley, the great conflict between Ulster and Connaught, which arose from the desire of Queen Medbh to own a bull to equal that of her husband Ailill.

The Fenian Cycle concerns the deeds of the hero Finn mac Cumhail and his warrior band, the Fianna. These include Finn's childhood, his encounter with Finn the Seer and the Salmon of Wisdom, and his pursuit of the lovers Diarmuid and Grainne. It also tells of his son Oisin, who was lured to the Land of Youth by the faerie Niamh, and how he eventually returned to Ireland after a lapse of three hundred years and after that lived long enough to regale St Patrick with the old hero tales of the Fianna.

The body of Welsh myth is less extensive and is mostly contained in the White Book of Rhydderch and the Red Book of Hergest. From these early books come the tales which were later included in the *Mabinogion* by Lady Charlotte Guest. The *Mabinogion* contains four main branches. These are the stories of Pwyll, Branwen, Manawydan and Math. Other tales include those of the early exploits of Arthur, and *Peredur*, which is one of the earliest accounts of the Holy Grail. The Book of Taliesin was also included in the *Mabinogion* by Lady Charlotte. The Welsh stories are very magical. They abound with magicians, spells, shapechanging and the transforming power of poetry. Their larger-than-life characters are considered to be euhemerised, or deified, versions of the original Welsh kings and nobles.

Although the monks began recording such tales as early as the sixth century CE, the earliest extant manuscripts date from the twelfth century. These are the Irish ones. The Welsh manuscripts date from the thirteenth century. However, as with the Irish tales, the myths contained in them are much earlier, having been passed down by oral tradition.

Information about Celtic belief comes from several sources. Archaeological discoveries show the importance of ritual, not least of which was the casting of precious objects into lakes as votive offerings to the gods. Figurines of deities have been found in springs, and huge richly carved stones, such as the Turoe stone in Ireland speak of outdoor rituals. Roman writings tell us that the Celts worshipped in the open air, in sacred places such as oak groves, and that they believed in the continued existence of the soul after death. But it is from the myths that we learn about their individual deities.

The Irish Book of Invasions tells of the coming of the faerie people, the Tuatha de Danann and it is from the Tuatha that the oldest gods derive, such as the Dagda, Boann and the Morrigan. The second generation of gods include Lugh, multi-skilled god of light, Aengus, god of love, and Brighid, goddess of fire, poetry and healing. However, the Celtic gods were much less clearly defined than those of the Romans. Their major deities often possessed several attributes, and there were numerous minor divinities connected with the land.

The land itself was embodied in the idea of the Goddess. She was synonymous with the Earth. She changed with the seasons and with the death and rebirth of the year. Triple goddess figures have been found in which the three women are depicted carrying flowers, fruit and possibly a withered branch. This conforms to the Celtic belief in the three aspects of the Goddess as maiden, mother and crone. Being so closely allied with nature, she was also considered the sovereign of the land. In the story of Niall, the Goddess appears in her hag form, but transforms into a beautiful maiden after receiving his love, and bestows on him the kingship of the land.

Celtic mythology abounds with stories concerning the union of the sovereign goddess and a king or hero. Such a union was believed to bestow fertility on the land and ensure its prosperity. Ceremonies of kingship included a ritual in which the king had intercourse with a white mare, representing the goddess, after which he drank a broth made from the mare's flesh. The idea of the sacrificial death and rebirth of the king which is found in Celtic myth is connected with the annual death and rebirth of the crops and vegetation. Triangular love stories also echo this theme. Tales such as that of Diarmuid and Grainne fleeing the wrath of Finn can be seen as symbolic of the young king contending with the old one for the hand of the Goddess. The defeat of the older by the younger man ensures the continuing fertility of the earth.

Being so closely allied with nature, the Goddess was also the holder of the powers of life and death. Some of the goddesses of Celtic myth, such as the Morrigan, are fearful and destructive, being connected with war and death. The dark face of the Goddess was an accepted part of life, and was considered as important as her light face. For the Celts acknowledged and respected the balance between death and life, dark and light, evil and good, believing that out of darkness came light, and out of death came life. Because of this, their day began with night, as the term "fortnight" (fourteen nights) attests, and their year with darkness. Thus, the festival of Samhain, the gateway to winter, marked the beginning of their year, which is why this book begins on 1 November.

The Celts were also very concerned with the yearly round and the ordering of the months, which they measured by means of the moon rather than the sun. The Coligny Calendar is the earliest Celtic calendar, dating from the first century BCE. It was once a large bronze plate but is now in fragments. It begins with the full moon of each month and divides the month into fortnights rather than weeks. Being lunar it inserted a short thirteenth month, a duplicate of Samonios, called Mid Samonios. Because the calendar was ruled by the full moon its dates were not fixed. The months ran as follows:

Samonios	October/November	Seed-fall
Dumannios	November/December	Darkest depths
Riuros	December/January	Cold-time
Anagantios	January/February	Stay-home time
Ogronios	February/March	Ice time
Cutios	March/April	Windy time
Giamonios	April/May	Shoots-show
Simivisonios	May/June	Bright time
Equos	June/July	Horse time
Elembiuos	July/August	Claim-time
Edrinios	August/September	Arbitration-time
Cantlos	September/October	Song-time

How To Use This Book

This is a circular book, reflecting the round of the seasons and the Celtic practices and beliefs that were inspired by the changing face of the land. The intention is that by dipping into the appropriate section for the time of year, and focusing on the individual passages and meditating on their content, the reader will be able to build up an understanding of the attitudes that informed Celtic society. An index is provided so that those who wish to follow a theme or storyline may easily do so. However, the full stories can be read elsewhere. The purpose of the extracts is to give glimpses of the myths and to point to some of the deeper meanings embedded within them.

At their deepest level the myths are often found to be intimately connected with the land. For example, the two women who feature in the story of Math represent, between them, the three seasonal aspects of the triple Goddess. Arianrhod, the virgin mother, represents her spring and summer aspects, while Blodeuwedd, the flowerbride who is turned into an owl, represents her summer and winter aspects. Different parts of the story, therefore, can be found in their appropriate season.

Other themes within the meditations include the magical attributes of the elements, Druidic training and belief, Celtic wit, the symbolic properties of number and colour, the sacred power of the word, the lure of the Otherworld, the divine power of love, the challenges of war and conflict, and the coming of Christianity. This last is reflected in the dialogues between Oisin and Cailte, two old Fenians who were said to have miraculously survived for three hundred years and were still alive when Patrick arrived in Ireland. The mutual respect and religious tensions recorded in the dialogues between the saint and the Fenians give a valuable insight into Druidic values at that time and offer much food for thought. A more poignant conflict appears in the Breton story of King Gradlon and Dahut in which the king is torn between his pagan daughter and his hermit friend.

Although it may seem strange to include the theme of war in a book of meditations, the Celts were a feisty people and laid so much store on fighting that they sometimes described it as one of the blessings of the Otherworld. Philosophically, too, they accepted pain and conflict alongside joy and achievement, much as they included dark with light and death with life. This dualistic attitude, although unpopular today, can at times offer a helpful perspective on life, especially in the face of difficulty.

Most of the meditations, however, concern the natural world, for the Celts believed above all in the interconnectedness of life and nature. They lived much closer to the earth than we do now, and their lives were governed by the turning of the seasons. Their bards also practised a very strict form of meditation when they lay in darkened chambers with stones on their bellies and reached down into the depths of their unconscious minds for the stirrings of inspiration, or when they slept on a hill or barrow and prepared themselves to receive knowledge of its history through dream.

Today more and more people are devising their own means of meditation. Although the revival of interest in this spiritual discipline initially came from eastern religions, many people in the West are discovering that there is much to draw on from the Western mystical tradition. Many also feel more comfortable with a Celtic-inspired spiritual practice because it is closer to home.

Celtic-style meditation primarily involves reconnecting with nature. At its most basic level this means spending more time in the countryside, especially in the summer months. Simply walking in the woods and fields or sitting quietly in a garden brings inner peace and harmony. Outside activities such as riding, swimming, sailing or running are health-giving on both a physical and spiritual level because they involve not only bodily exercise but also a direct connection with the elements. Because this connection is so important, many who practise indoor meditation find it helpful to set up a small table with a candle and a selection of objects to symbolise the elements, seasons and directions (see page 162).

In Celtic ritual, the powers of the four seasons are invoked and the gates to the four directions opened for such powers to come in. Participants are encouraged to recognise and honour the elements and directions and take wisdom from the animals, birds, and deities associated with them. These rituals can be carried out alone but are often easier and more effective in a group. For a more personal and solitary experience, let your imagination lead you into the Celtic Otherworld. You might like to light a candle or listen to Celtic harp music whilst visualising your journey in this rejuvenating land. You may find the Well of Wisdom there and take a drink from it, or you may meet the Goddess in one of her aspects. This type of visualisation need only take a few minutes but is a simple and effective form of Celtic-inspired meditation.

Although some people prefer to work alone, many prefer to work with others, and for them there are several Celtic spiritual groups in existence. Some groups meet regularly to celebrate the quarterly festivals, solstices and equinoxes. Others make it their task to discover and restore ancient wells and springs. Many explore the myths in order to deepen their understanding or to reflect on the gods and goddesses, who are regarded in Celtic understanding as aspects of an undefined divinity. Above all, the genuine Druidic or Celtic groups are careful to respect the individual spiritual understanding and beliefs of their members. A list of some of these organisations is given at the back of this book.

The proliferation of such groups shows that there are many people at this time who wish to deepen their understanding of the Celts and partake of their wisdom. Because the Celtic approach to life is so different from ours, it is only by tasting their stories, their beliefs and their magic and by contemplating their reverence for all natural and animal life, that their wise and challenging view of the world can be experienced. This book is written in the hope that all who look for new inspiration and spiritual sustenance will find it in this rich and ancient heritage of a remarkable and gifted people.

WINTER

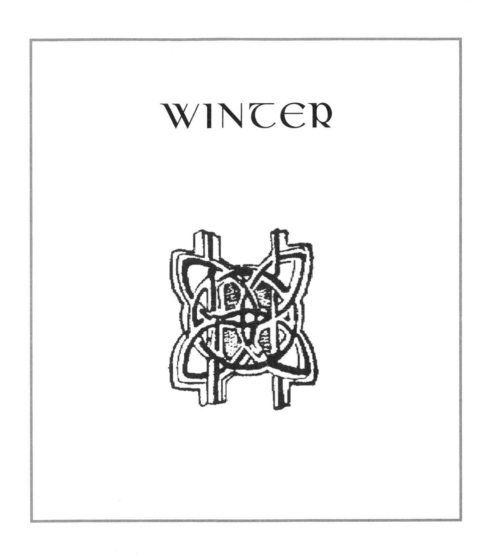

AMHAIN, pronounced "Sowain," means "Summer's end." It was a lunar festival held at the time of the full moon at the end of October and marking the Celtic New Year. It lasted for about a week and corresponds to our modern-day celebrations of Hallowe'en and All Hallows. In fact, many of the rituals attached to Hallowe'en come from the ancient festival of Samhain. The Celts believed that at this crucial point of the year when the earth turned away from light and began to embrace the darkness, the doors to the Otherworld were opened and the veil between this world and the realm of spirit all but disappeared. Then the holy men and those who had prepared themselves were able to communicate with the spirits of the ancestors. This was considered an opportunity to reconnect with past loved ones, a time to learn from their instruction and guidance and to commune with the next world. As time went on, the belief grew up that some of

Samhain

the spirits released at this time could be angry or malevolent. Rituals of appeasement or protection were devised, and the practice arose of "saining" or blessing foods and objects that might be contaminated by such evil spirits. In Celtic Christian times, this idea was turned into All Saints Day, the day which drew down the purifying power and blessing of the saints to combat the release of the powers of darkness.

For the ancient Celts, however, the festival of Samhain stood at the gateway of winter, the time of coldness and death, the season ruled by the Cailleach, the old hag, dark face of the triple goddess. But it was also the time of the wisdom of the Old Crone, a time to consider the past and plan for the future, an opportunity to deepen spiritual understanding. It was the season to rest from outward activity, to go inwards and work on the spirit, or simply to withdraw and conserve energy in order to become renewed and invigorated in the spring, like the crops themselves.

Celtic lunar festivals were deeply connected with the agricultural round of the seasons and with the movement of cattle. At Samhain herds of cattle and other livestock were brought into shelters for the winter, while the weaker animals were slaughtered and salted in preparation for the great feasts. All the harvest had to be gathered in by this time, anything remaining in the fields being forfeit to the Cailleach. The season of darkness and apparent death was greatly revered, for it was understood that at this time the forces of nature were working particularly potently within the element of earth, empowering the seeds and grain and preparing them for germination in the spring.

The festival of Samhain also symbolically reflected the phase when the moon was absent, the days of complete blackness. This was the origin of the idea of timelessness and of the suspension of rule and order, which gave rise to the three days of "misrule." At this time men and women exchanged clothes, practical jokes were enacted, cattle were moved from one farm to another, and children went round the neighbouring dwellings asking for gifts and food and threatening mischief if they were not placated. This ritual survives today in the Hallowe'en custom of "trick or treating."

This was also the time of the great Assembly of Tara. Every three years all the chiefs and nobles of Ireland gathered at the High King's court to discuss and ratify the laws of the land. While the Assembly was being held, all violence, stealing or legal disputes were strictly forbidden, on pain of death. The Assembly was held at Samhain because this was the time when warring ceased between tribes. During the winter months Celtic warriors desisted from fighting and hunting and instead were billeted on various households where they spent their days feasting and being entertained by music and storytelling. Among those who had received a Druidic training, riddling exchanges took place, in which meanings were conveyed on more than one level. At this time, too, plans were made for tribal alliances or for necessary warfare.

Although the cold and darkness may have seemed harsh to a people who were closely involved with the land, as the season approached its shortest day they began to prepare for the most important celebration of the year, the festival marking the rebirth of the sun after its sojourn in death and darkness. This was the midwinter solstice, the first of the fire festivals. The great tomb at Newgrange is constructed with a special aperture for the first rays of the sun to shine through at the solstice and light the inner chamber. Behind this solar festival, which took place at the heart of the season of winter, lay the belief in the ritual of the death of the king, consort of the Great Goddess, who in herself represented all of Nature. Annually, at the turning point of the year, she demanded the sacrifice of the king, her consort. Like the vegetation itself, he had to die before becoming resurrected with the rising of the newborn sun on 22 December. This concept also underlies the battle between the Oak King and the Holly King. At midwinter, the Holly King defeats the Oak, and at Midsummer, the Oak King wrests the crown back from the Holly.

Alongside the holly, all evergreen trees were considered particularly sacred at this time. Holly and ivy were paired symbolically in terms of masculine and feminine forces, and mistletoe was given particular reverence as the plant that descended from the heavens and germinated in the upper branches of the oak, the sacred tree of the Celts. The annual ritual of cutting the mistletoe from a ring of oaks, a sacred Druidic grove, has been described in detail by the Roman writer Pliny. This was performed at the winter solstice, the mistletoe being cut by a golden sickle and let fall onto a white sheet. After this, two white bulls were sacrificed to the gods, and prayers given for the renewed fertility of the earth. The mistletoe was not allowed to touch the ground, for it was the gift of regeneration from the god of the heavens.

Although some of the rituals and sacrifices may seem primitive, in many ways Celtic spiritual understanding was very sophisticated. For the Celts, darkness came before light and death before life, for they perceived this to be the nature of reality. No new life could be achieved without the experience of death, nor could light be appreciated without the corresponding power of darkness. Thus, their year began with the time of death and darkness, the time of engendering, the time of gestation when the child was nurtured in the womb of the mother, the seed in the womb of Great Mother Earth. This was the beginning of all things.

The meditations for this season focus on the themes of darkness and spiritual renewal, the element of earth and its related symbolism, the Cailleach and Wise Crone aspect of the Goddess, the sacred properties of evergreen trees and winter-hardy animals, bardic training, the power of the word, the language of Ogham, heroic feasting and riddling, tales of love and death, and nature poems. Meditating on such stories, descriptions and symbols will give us an insight into the mystical Celtic understanding of the gifts and challenges of this season.

THE OATH OF THE ELEMENTS

If I break faith with you,
may the skies fall upon me,
may the seas drown me,
may the earth rise up and swallow me.

THE SACRED ELEMENT OF EARTH

Sacred element of earth, Nature, the land itself, all-powerful realm of the Great Mother. Nurturer and very ground of being, you raise up life and swallow death. Out of your womb comes rebirth and renewal. Springs of living water are engendered in you. Furrowed one and seed-receiver, fertile one of copious harvest, sweet-bosomed nourisher of men. Green-mantled, braided with yellow corn, lake-eyed, hill-breasted, bounteous maiden. Mystical are your caves, your dark and secret dwellings, unseen wisdom in their blackness. Mound-shaper of the *sidhe*, mysterious gateway to the Otherworld, and hider of the dead. Keeper of unknown powers and undiscovered riches. Hoarder of wealth and precious metals, holder of potent minerals. Deepest one of greatest blessing, sustainer of life, promoter of sense and touch, material wealth and grounding, north is your direction and the sacred stone your symbol.

SACRED STONES

Lia Fail, Stone of Kings,
Stone that shrieks aloud when kings ascend it
Stone that shrieked when Cormac stood on it
Stone of the earth, the land and Sovereignty,
Gift of the Tuatha.

The magical gift relating to the element of earth is the Stone of Destiny which was brought to Ireland by the faerie people, the Tuatha de Danann. It was known as the *Lia Fail*, or Stone of Fal. It stood on the Hill of Tara beside the Great Palace of the High Kings of Ireland. It had oracular powers and cried out when the rightful king ascended it. Standing stones of all kinds were sacred to the druids. The ancient stone circles, such as those of Stonehenge and Avebury, although built by an earlier people, were probably used by druids as temples for their rituals. Standing stones connect with powerful earth energies and were used for the swearing of oaths. The cult of the stone was also connected with healing. Water blessed and poured over a stone and then collected was used as a purifying medicine. Passing a child through a hole in a stone denoted both healing and spiritual rebirth. The druids famously carried magical "snakestones" which may have given rise to the "Philosopher's Stone" in alchemy.

Winter

The colour has drained from the lake
the keen frost covers it,
the grass stands stiffly, each blade frozen,
the stags are lowing on the hills
searching the ice-rimed twigs for food
the eagle cries in plaintive misery
his beak pearl-beaded.

HOLLY

Holly was known as *tinne* in old Irish/gaelic, meaning "fire" and it is linked with this element. It was a holy tree, evergreen, tenacious, a symbol of immortality. It was especially potent at midwinter when it had won the crown from the oak tree and began its half-yearly reign. At this season it could be taken into the home, both to perpetuate the powers of nature within it and to bring in elves and faeries at a time when their presence was believed to be beneficial to mortals. However, every last stick of greenery had to be removed by the festival of Imbolc in case the elementals decided to remain in the house and cause mischief. The holly king was originally the Wildman or spirit of vegetation, later called the Green Man.

Holly tree, holy tree
with green leaves so bright
at the waning of the year
you bring in the light.

Holly tree, holy tree
with berries so red
at the waning of the year
you wake from the dead.

Holly tree, holy tree
with blossom so white
at the waning of the year
you bring us new hope.

Holly tree, holy tree
with your bitter bark
at the waning of the year
you save us from the dark.

THE ORDER OF BARD

*'The Bards sang to the sweet strains of the lyre the valorous deeds of
famous men composed in heroic verse."*
(AMMIANUS)

The bards believed the Truth was enshrined in the Word and the Word was
sacred. They were forbidden to write anything down and, instead, com-
mitted thousands of lines to memory, becoming keepers of the history and
genealogy of their people. They also studied various poetic forms, gram-
mar, oration and the ogham alphabet. Bardic colleges were harsh places,
devoid of comfort or sensory delight. In order to invoke inner powers, they
spent long hours underground lying in the dark with stones on their chests
"searching into secret and sublime things" while powerful images danced
before them and poems rose up in their minds. After twelve years, when a
bard was sufficiently trained, he travelled around, telling stories to the
sounds of the harp. First he shook a silver or gold branch hung with bells
to summon the magical spirits to help him; then, striking a chord on the
harp, he would begin:

"When on a summer morning early the curly-bearded chief arises for the
deer-hunt, there is dew on the grass, the blackbird warbling, and the life
has gone out of the frost . . ."

The Splendour of King Cormac

A splendid figure of a king was Cormac.
Except for Conair, Conchobor or Aengus Og himself,
none could rival him in beauty.
Noble he was, with yellow braided hair;
he held a red shield on his arm engraved with gold.
A purple cloak was folded on his shoulder;
a jewelled brooch was on his breast; about his neck he wore
a golden torc; his shirt was white, and round his waist
he had a golden girdle set with precious jewels.
Two gold-clasped shoes he wore, two sharp spears
ringed with gold he held in his right hand.
Fair was his form, unblemished; in his head
he had a shower of teeth like pearls, his mouth
was red as rowan berries, white his skin
as purest snow, his body well-formed, and his cheek
soft as the mountain foxglove. His two eyes
were bright as bluebells while his brows and lashes shone
sharp as a blue-black blade. Thus fair and noble
Cormac the High King entered the Hall of Tara
to lead the Great Assembly of the men of Erin.

FINN'S BETROTHAL FEAST

There was a great feast held at Tara in the court of Cormac mac Art, the High King of Ireland. It was held in honour of the betrothal of his daughter the princess Grainne to Finn mac Cumhail, the hoary-headed captain of the brave warriors of the Fianna. While they were eating and drinking in the Great Hall, Finn began speaking to Grainne in the Druid tongue. Now there was this about Finn, that he was wise with an Otherworldly wisdom which he had got from the cup of the sidhe, and powers of far-sightedness that he had got from shutting his thumb in the doorway of a mound of the *sidhe*. For this reason, having lost his first wife, he had difficulty in finding another who could equal him in wit and wisdom. For Finn had vowed that he would only marry a woman who could answer all his questions and, indeed, there were few who could answer them. But Grainne was a woman not only of great beauty but also of wisdom and Druidical knowledge, and equal to any test that he might give her.

THE POWER OF THE WORD

After spending long years of training in the Bardic Colleges, and having mastered the sacred word and learned to order its pattern and command its maximum potency, the bard was eventually able to use its power magically. This ability was mostly employed to praise patrons or record glorious deeds and battles but sometimes it was used to curse. The curse of a bard or druid was particularly feared because, by composing a satire or *glam dicin* a bard could ruin a king. For example, lack of hospitality was sufficient reason for the bard Corpry to conjure boils on King Bres, by this means forcing him, as a blemished king, to abdicate. In a contest between two bards, Nede tells Ferchetne about the arts he practises:

> The answer is not hard:
> blushing of countenance,
> flesh-wounding satire,
> raising up bashfulness
> exposing shamelessness,
> promoting poetry,
> seeking fame,
> fostering science …
> composing poems
> in a small chamber,
> abundance of teaching,
> telling of tales and delighting kings.

FINN'S TESTING OF GRAINNE

While they feasted Finn began to question Grainne.

"Tell me," he said, "what is more numerous than the blades of grass?"

"That is easy, my lord, the drops of dew outnumber the blades of grass."

"And what is it that burns more fiercely than the fire?

"That, again, is easy. A woman's choosing between two men."

"What runs faster than the wind?"

"A woman's thinking between two men."

"For what is there no lock or chain?"

"The eye of a man who looks on his friend."

"What is of a redder hue than blood?"

"The face of a man who has no meat to offer strangers.

"What is sharper than a sword?"

"The reproach of an enemy."

"What is the most valuable jewel?"

"A knife."

"What has more softness than down."

"The touch of a palm on a lover's cheek."

"What is the worthiest of deeds?"

"A high deed that carries no arrogance."

"What is blacker than the raven?"

"There is death."

"And what is whiter than snow?

"There is truth."

After that Finn was satisfied, but Grainne herself was not. For, quicker indeed than the wind itself, was the darting of her thoughts between hoary-headed Finn, the great Captain of the Fianna, and Diarmuid of the Love-spot, the fairest of Finn's men.

THE DRUID'S SNAKESTONE

Druids were sometimes called *Naddred*, or "adders." Their magical energy was bound up with the energy of the snake. The symbol of the double snake indicated its dual qualities of death and rebirth, poison and healing, destructive and productive energies. On sacred phallic-shaped druidic altars, such as have been found in Cumbria and Gloucestershire, there are carvings of a snake holding an egg in its mouth, or coiled round an egg or stone. This potent depiction of fertility and conception is translated into a symbol of spiritual regeneration in the magical properties of the Druid's snakestone or *glain neidre*. This mysterious object, described by Pliny as being formed by snake saliva, was one of their magic talismans, used for healing. There has been speculation that it may have been an ancient fossil or a gem of some kind. But whatever its origins it was undoubtedly connected with the extraordinary powers of the snake as an Underworld guardian of deep and ancient regenerative and secret knowledge.

THE POWER OF THE MOON

Luminous, shape-shifting jewel of the night. Goddess of changes, silver-sickled maiden, full-bodied mother, waning crone. Dweller in three-day death and darkness, rising chalice of rebirth, bestower of fertility. Light-reflecting one of inner contemplative knowledge, sky-wanderer, drawing on power of waves. Earth-mirror, trailer of Otherworldly light, enricher of hidden life and mystic one of subtle energy. Tranquil sky-boat, bestower of dreams, in harmony with the ebb and flow of life. Wisdom of ancient knowing shines from you, gift-giver, lighter of the soul.

> Hail to you, moon-bright goddess
> form-changing subtle enchantress,
> you cut the sky with your silver sickle
> drawing the current of the sea behind you.
>
> Hail, white maiden moon,
> Hail, red, full-blooded mother,
> Hail, black empty one of death,
> Hail slender, new-birthed virgin.

ASPECTS OF THE GODDESS—THE CAILLEACH OR CRONE

The Goddess had three aspects, Maiden, Mother and Crone. Because she was the embodiment of the land itself, her Crone aspect manifested itself in winter when the earth was bare and the crop-seeds, hidden underground, appeared to die. But, as the seeds themselves testify, in darkness and apparent death lies mystical sustenance and regeneration. The Celts recognised the power and necessity of this death-dealing and destructive aspect of the Great Mother because they realised that her destructiveness encompassed a more positive challenging aspect. As their myths demonstrate, being challenged by the Dark Goddess was an essential part of every hero's journey. The Old Crone, or Wise One, although being the dark side of the Great Mother, was indispensable just as night is to day and dark is to light.

I am the Dark One
old as time itself,
Giver of Life and Taker
I have many names.
Black Annis, Gyre Carlin
or the Hag of Beare.

I am the Witch of Winter
and my face is blue.
Men fear me
old and withered as I am
for I hold death in my hand.

I am the Challenger
I stand in the road
confronting all who come.

I am the wise one,
death is in my hand,
but in my other hand
is life.

Queen Medbh Chooses a Husband

Queen Medbh of Connaught was given a province of Ireland by her father to govern, and she ruled it from Cruachu. Many suitors came to ask for her hand, the sons of kings, captains and famous warriors, all offering her wealth, gifts and land. But Medbh said she required a harder marriage-price than all these. What she looked for was the lack of three things in her suitor, namely meanness, fear and jealousy. Regarding meanness, Medbh declared that she herself was so generous that it would be a great inequality to be wedded to a man who was mean and close-handed. Regarding fear, she said that it would be insulting to have a timid husband when she herself was so spirited and thrived on trouble. And regarding jealousy, she declared that she had never yet enjoyed a man without there being another waiting in his shadow. For this reason she chose Ailill, the son of Rus Ruad of Leinster, for she perceived that there was no meanness, fear or jealousy in him.

Gwydion Punishes Blodeuwedd

Blodeuwedd was fleeing with her maidens, fearing the wrath of Gwydion. Her maidens ran backwards, fell into a lake and were drowned, leaving Blodeuwedd to face Gwydion alone. When he came up with her he seized hold of her and said:

"I will not kill you for I have a worse fate for you. You shall become a creature of the dark, never daring to show your face in daylight from this day onwards. If you do, you will be mobbed and attacked by other birds, for you shall become an owl, the most feared and hated of all birds. And you shall keep your name and for ever be called Blodeuwedd."

Then as she stared at him in terror, her mouth became pointed, her eyes round and yellow and her cheeks wild and feathered. When her transformation was complete, she raised her wings and flew into the night sky.

Sacred Symbols—The Square

Being four-sided, the square symbolised the balance of opposites, and the order of the universe. Accordingly, the Celts venerated the four directions, the four seasons, and the four elements. They believed these demonstrated the properties of the earth and were forces which, held in balance, promoted and sustained material life and gave stability to mortal existence. The square with its four equal sides was, to them, the symbol of matter, earthly reality and mankind. The balance of opposites contained in the square was also believed to represent the dual nature of reality, of light and darkness, good and evil, life and death, destruction and renewal.

This fourfold division of the manifest world was often used in multiples, for example there were eight seasonal festivals, and eight mystical winds, or *airts*. In Celtic thinking, the even numbers symbolised the natural world, while the odd numbers denoted the unseen, spiritual world. However, the natural world was not considered inferior to the Otherworld; the Celts had as much respect for the laws of nature and the stable element of earth as for the other more mystical elements.

The Dragon of the Earth

Dragons are found in myths worldwide. They symbolise states of being and share the attributes of the elements. The dragon connected with the element of earth is a guardian of treasure—the treasure of the soul. A clear distinction must be made between hoarding and guarding, for the dragon must not prevent the use of such treasure, only the stealing of it by others. The inner dragon is thus a protector of inner riches. It is depicted either as guarding a cave, a faerie or burial mound, or a hill. It is a type of the serpent who famously coils round the World Tree, showing its connection with the roots of life. In ancient heroic tales the hero has to overcome the dragon in order to have access to the wealth it guards. Dragons also guard or threaten women, and need to be overcome by the hero for the release of his soul.

Dragon of Earth
guardian of gold,
the jewel-bright hoard,
and wealth of the soul.

Fierce, fiery one,
root-holding, gift-giving,
you yield the brave warrior
the treasure within.

THE EARTH CASTS UP CIAN

Cian, the father of Lugh, saw the three Sons of Turenn approaching him. He took the form of a wild boar and entered a herd of swine to hide himself. But the Sons of Turenn saw him and changed into hounds and drove him out. Then one of them cast a spear at him at which he cried out: "Do not kill me in the shape of a pig!"

"Return to your own shape, then!" they replied.

Cian became a man again and said: "Look at me now, my face is blooded. You knew only too well who I was, oath-breakers that you are!"

"Take back your insult," they shouted, but Cian refused, saying that if they dared to kill him his blood would cry out against them. Being now in great anger, the Sons of Turenn stoned him to death. Afterwards they built a grave for him which was as deep as the man was high. But when they had laid him in it and covered him over, the earth cast him up again. Six times they tried to bury him and six times the earth cast him up again, but on the seventh, the earth remained still with Cian under it.

SLIEVE GUA

Place of darkness and wolf-wandering
storm-hollowed, ravaged by rough winds,
wolf-howls echo in your chasms.
The brown deer in autumn
bells in your cold ravines,
the crane's harsh cry
cracks over your frost-hard crags.

THE SEARCH FOR MABON

When the task was put on Arthur and his warriors to find Mabon, son of Modron, who was taken from his mother while still a baby, they went first to enquire of the most ancient of birds, the Ousel of Cilgwri. The Ousel said that though he had worn away the anvil of a smith by pecking it with his beak every day, yet in all that time he had heard nothing of the Mabon. He sent them to the Stag of Redynvyre, who said that although he had remained alive long enough to watch an oak tree grow from sapling to full strength and die again, he had heard nothing of the Mabon. He, in turn, sent them to the Owl of Cwm Cawlwyd, who said that though he had lived through the growth and decay of three woods, yet he too knew nothing of the Mabon. The Owl sent them to the Eagle of Gwern Abwy, who said that even though he had pecked at a rock daily, reducing it from a great height to a mere span, yet he, also, knew nothing of the Mabon. He sent them to the Salmon of Llyn Llyw, the oldest creature living, and the salmon said: "Every tide I go upriver as far as the walls of Gloucester, and there I have discovered a great wrong." Then the salmon took two of the knights, one on each shoulder and carried them to the wall. They heard a loud noise of lamenting coming from inside, so Arthur gathered all the warriors of the land and broke through the prison wall and released the sacred child, the Mabon.

THE WISE OWL

The owl, or *Cailleach-oidhche*, meaning "Cailleach of the Night," is linked with the Old Crone, or Wise Woman, the third aspect of the Goddess. A lunar creature, sun-hating, the owl has opposing characteristics to those of the eagle. Wisdom and intuitive knowledge of the occult powers are its sacred attributes. To work with the owl is to delve into hidden mysteries and to come close to the Otherworld and the boundaries of death itself.

The Owl of Cawlwyd is one of the totem beasts consulted in the story of the Seeking of Mabon. It appears well down the chain of older creatures, only the Eagle and the Salmon being more ancient. Like the Cailleach herself, the owl was once respected for its wisdom and its role as a threshold guardian. During later Christian times it became feared as a bird of ill omen. In the story of Math, the nature goddess Blodeuwedd is turned into an owl by Gwydion for betraying her husband Lleu. Although this is depicted as a punishment in the story, it shows the Goddess entering her Crone phase.

Far-seeing, round-
eyed, fierce-beaked,
crouching Cailleach,
your wild call
wakes the spirits
of night-walkers.
Wary, wizened,
Guardian of Death's
threshold.
Feathered
holder of
older
wisdom,
watching,
waiting ...

MIDWINTER SOLSTICE

21 December

At the dark point of the year, the threshold of the ancient tomb is wrapped in night. Journey down its narrow passage, emerging in the stillness of the pitch-black chamber. Meditate on the power of death and hidden mysteries and await the dawn, the time of wonder. As the first wavering beam strikes through the opening, illumining the chamber, intricate carvings, patterns, spirals of infinity, solar circlings suddenly appear on stony walls and ceiling. Now the year has reached its turning. Blessed return of light, ray of the sun-god, symbol of hope, proclaimer of life, the season's rebirth. Mabon, the young son, is born again, the light of spirit quenches the power of darkness. Light candles, burn Yule logs, gather green holly, ivy, mistletoe, the plants of hope and everlasting life, and crown the world tree with a heavenly star, the shining promise of new birth and spiritual awakening.

CELTIC PATTERNS

The Celts believed that everything in the natural world was interconnected. Their ovates and druids could shapeshift and partake of animal nature, their gods and goddesses could change into animal and bird familiars. The flowing of a river, the tumble of a waterfall, the whispering of two leaves together, the soaring of a flock of birds—all these had meaning and, if understood correctly, could illumine other happenings in the world. Appearance and reality were symbolically linked and the artwork of the Celts was often fluid like their beliefs. Unbroken lines ran into unending spirals creating patterns which flowed into human and animal forms and out again, symbolising eternal life. Curving abstract lines adorned wheels, mirrors, ornaments or shields, expressing the continuity of all reality, manifest or hidden, whether seen with the mortal eye or the eye of inner vision.

THE MISTLETOE ON THE OAK

The most sacred winter solstice ceremony of the Druids was that of cutting down mistletoe that had alighted on an oak, as if falling from the heavens. Known as All-heal and believed to carry the seed of life, it was ritually lopped using a golden sickle. The mistletoe was not allowed to touch the ground but was caught in a pure white cloth and taken to the sacred altar. After this, two white bulls were sacrificed. The whole ceremony marked the ritual fertilisation of the earth-goddess by the god of the sky, who laid his seed, symbolised by the white berries of the mistletoe, on the bare branches of the oak. This rare hosting of the mistletoe by the oak denoted the great Godhead drawing near to the earth and embracing all mortality. The golden sickle was a combined symbol of sun and moon. The mistletoe branch, like that of the apple, was a type of mystical Silver Branch used by the Druids to summon the powers of the Otherworld.

O Drui of wisdom
bearer of the white-berried dancer –
the sacred one
who descends from the sky
clothing the oaks.

No leaf or berry
touches the earth
while the sickle of gold
severs the green stems
and the white bulls wait.

Blessings on you
who carry to the Great Mother
the pearl-bright seeds
of the young god.

THE SACRED BULL, OR *TARBH*

The attributes of the sacred bull are these: strength, fertility and prosperity. At the winter solstice it was necessary to sacrifice two white bulls at the ritual cutting of the mistletoe. Two famous magic bulls, the White-horned of Connaught and the Brown of Cuailnge in Ulster, lie at the heart of the story of the Cattle Raid of Cooley, both bulls originally being shape-changing humans. The bull-skin was considered magical and the Celts practised a shamanic form of divination, the *tarbh feis*, in which a druid drank the broth made from a newly killed bull and ate its flesh. After that he lay down on its skin, guarded by awen, or watchers, and prepared to be given a dream or vision concerning the whole tribe. This ritual was also used for the choosing of a king, who would appear to the druid in his dream. The bull was symbolically connected with the king, representing his power, his fertility, and the prosperity of his kingdom.

THE OAK IN WINTER

King of the forest, father of trees
Bare branches antlering the winter sky
thick-boled, reclothing at midsummer.
But at winter solstice harbouring like snow —
rare visitation, god's fertility —
white-berried mistletoe.

TRISTAN AND ISEULT

King Mark, who was Arthur's cousin, went to Arthur to ask him to settle the matter of his wife's infidelity with Tristan. Arthur accordingly sent harpers and storytellers to King Mark's court with the intention of lulling him into a mood of reconciliation. Mark paid the bards handsomely, but when they were gone his grievance returned. Then Arthur called Mark and Tristan before him and offered Iseult to the one man for half a year and afterwards to the other. Giving King Mark the choice he asked him: "Do you wish to have Iseult when the leaves are upon the trees or when they are not?" Mark said at once that he would rather have her when the leaves were not on the trees for then the nights were longer. At this Iseult sprang up with gladness in her eyes and ran to Tristan. "My lord," she said, "then will you have me all the year." After that she composed an *englyn*:

> These three trees my champions be
> the holly, the yew and the ivy
> for while they keep their greenery
> I shall have my love beside me.

THE YEW TREE

The yew, or *ioho*, is one of the oldest trees. It is evergreen and powerful and bears poisonous berries. It is frequently seen in graveyards and has long been associated both with death and regeneration. The Celts believed that it reached its roots down into the bones of the dead and manifested their spirits. In the tragic stories of dying lovers, it was often the yew tree that grew out of their graves and joined them with its branches. Because it was so hardy and durable it was used to make coffins and weapon handles. Also, druids carved ogham script onto yew rods and used them for divination. Being so long-lived, the yew became a symbol of eternity and was connected with the wheel of the seasons. At one time, this symbolic wheel was depicted on the High King's brooch to remind him of his duty towards the lasting health of the realm.

Ioho, ancient, poisonous, venerable,
one of the Five Magic trees of Eire
you blend with graves but yet
endure. Out of the bony mouths
of skeletons you speak
and join the branchy arms
of lovers after death
Deirdre and Naoise,
Tristan and Iseult.
You speak in ogham.
Druids carve their symbols on your rods
and strew your branches on the ground
to give their prophecies. The sun god
honours you, O great one,
Spell of Knowledge
and the High King's wheel.

OGHAM

The Druids regarded the power of the word as sacred, so stories and magical lore had to be memorised, for it was forbidden to write them down. The Druids did, however, use a code that they carved onto standing stones or wooden wands. This was a symbolic alphabet composed of different numbers of strokes bisecting a central line. The number of strokes to the left or right of it, and the angle at which they were carved, indicated the different letters. The script was known as Ogham (O'am). It is thought that the letters represented groupings from the natural world, such as trees, animals, birds and rivers.

The most well-known construction of the script is Tree Ogham, in which the letters are allied to tree-names. In this method the first five trees are represented by groups of one, two, three, four and five strokes to the right of the vertical line. The following five trees are similarly represented to the left of it. Further letters are indicated by slanting strokes across the line, and finally by horizontal strokes across it, making twenty letters in all. Ogham is believed to have been one of the chief tools of communication between druids, acting as a storehouse of encoded knowledge.

Sacred Numbers—One

The number One stands for original unity, undivided first principle and ancient spirituality. Its properties are most clearly depicted in the figures of the oldest deities in Celtic myths. For example, the giant Lord of the Animals who appears in *Owein* has one leg and one eye. Figures possessing only one limb inhabit another dimension, an odd or occult dimension, and operate through Otherworldly powers. One-legged deities are extremely ancient and of chthonic origin. Such giant figures often had only one eye, examples include Ysbaddaden in Welsh myth, Balor, his Irish counterpart, and Sharvan the Surly, guardian of the Quicken Tree. Having one eye denoted the power of second sight, though in primitive form. Loss of a limb or organ was often thought to confer increased spiritual power, as in the belief that the blind seer was gifted with greater inner vision.

The Druidic posture for cursing was to stand on one leg, hold out one arm and close one eye. In this way the Druids invoked the concentrated power of the old ferocious nature gods. The sun-god Lugh adopted this pose when cursing the enemy during the Battle of Mag Tuiread.

COLD IS THE NIGHT

Cold is the night on the Great Moor,
the rain pours down, no trifle;
a roar in which the clean wind rejoices
howls over the sheltering wood.

A WRETCHED LIFE

A wretched life it is living in the wild. Dear God! To have no house for shelter, to drink nothing but water from the stream and to have only the stringy, green-haired watercress for food. Sleeping in knotty branches in the tops of trees, and falling out, then wandering for hours through scratchy gorse. Shunning human company, keeping only with the wild wolf or racing the brown stag on the bare plain. No soft and downy covering to keep me warm at night, alone in the tree's crown with no comfort, no human voice for company, Oh Christ, what grief! I can run easily up the mountain—few can match my vigour. Even so, my looks are all gone, which were once unparalleled amongst men. Oh God, what wretchedness!

Maeldun Comes to the Island of Wailing

They came to an island and saw on it a host of black men clad in black clothes and hoods. And the men were continually wailing, and seemed unable to cease from their lament. Then, drawing lots, it fell to one of Maeldun's foster-brothers to venture onto the island. So he went ashore, but as soon as he came up to the men he himself began wailing with them. Then Maeldun instructed four of his men to go and rescue him. He cautioned them neither to look at the ground nor to breathe the air when they were on the island. So the men wrapped their clothes around their noses and mouths and kept their eyes fixed on their comrade. In this way and by using force they rescued him. After that, Maeldun asked what had caused such lament on the island. The man replied that he did not know, except that he saw what the men saw while he was among them.

BLACK IS THE LAKE

Black is the lake, deep cold its bed,
the reed stems shiver
while the frost-fringed branches of the trees
crack on the hard ground.
Winter has hurled its spear
and bound the ploughed fields
in mail-hard ice and darkness.

PEREDUR AND THE
HOARY-HAIRED KNIGHT

The hoary-headed man was sitting by the fire when Peredur entered. He invited the young boy to sit by him. They ate a meal and then the man asked the boy if he was a good swordsman. Peredur said he was skilled in fighting with a stick and a shield. The man commanded his two sons to fight him with sticks and shields. Peredur struck one of them and wounded him above the eye. Then the hoary-haired man held up his hand. "You may cease now," he said, "for you have proved yourself and you will indeed be a skilled swordsman, the best in the land."

Then the man told Peredur that he was his uncle and would undertake to instruct him. He said, moreover, that he would teach him manners, for the lad was uncouth, and would afterwards make him a knight. Then the man gave Peredur this advice: he told him that whatever he might see, however strange the thing seemed to him, he should refrain from asking about it but should wait to be told its meaning. And that was the reason Peredur let the Grail pass by in silence.

Symbolic Colours—Black

Black is one of the three mystical Celtic colours, the others being red and white. When Deirdre sees a raven drinking calf's blood on the snow, she has a vision of a man with hair as black as the raven, skin as white as snow and cheeks as red as blood. She falls under the spell of this image, which leads to her elopement with Naoise. In the *Mabinogion*, Peredur has a similar vision concerning his wife. Black, being associated with the raven, was also associated with death. The raven was the totem bird of the Morrigan, goddess of death. She would appear in battle, foretelling the death of warriors and sometimes settling on their shoulders in raven form, as she did with Cuchulainn after he died. Black was also associated with ancient and primitive beings, such as the black Lord of the Beasts encountered by Owein in Welsh myth.

Deirdre Looks out across the Icy Landscape

Against the snow she saw,
black upon white, a raven
drinking the red blood from a calf fresh-killed.
"That is the man I want," said Deirdre, "with hair
blacker than raven's feathers, limbs
whiter than untouched snow, and cheeks
redder than new-spilled blood.
Tell me if such a man is living?"
"Yes," said her guardian Levarcham,
"there is such a man, a champion,
one of the Sons of Usna,
taller by a head than both his brothers.
His name is Naoise."

The Serpent of Rebirth

The serpent or snake was a highly venerated symbol of female energies and of chthonic wisdom and rebirth. The shedding of its skin represented regeneration; its burrowing in the earth, and slipping into crevices in dark places, caves and rocks, showed its affinity with the great Earth Mother. Like the dragon, or great Worm, it encircled the World Tree, guarding ancient mysteries. It was traditionally believed to lie and speak truth simultaneously with its forked tongue. A potent symbol of sexuality, it also possessed an ancient feminine wisdom that was considered healing and beneficent.

Skin-shedding serpent
messenger of death
and rebirth. Wizened, coiling one
of ancient knowing, chthonic,
servant of earth's
deepest energies. The Mother
nurtures you, O cunning
double-tongued deceiver
flickering truth and lies,
wisdom and wiliness.
Soul-healer, sensual
inner guardian,
life-conceiver.

PEREDUR'S REVERIE

While Arthur and his men were searching for him, Peredur was arrested by a sight that held him as if by a spell. In front of the hermit's cell where he had spent the night, was a spatter of three colours. A duck was lying on the snow, the kill of a hawk, dropped when it was disturbed, and a raven was perched on the duck. All at once the whiteness of the snow, the black of the raven and the red of the blood conjured for Peredur the face of the woman who was to him his own soul. Peredur became so overwhelmed at the thought of her, and was so lost in his reverie that when Kei approached him Peredur heard nothing until that contentious knight cast his spear at him. Then Peredur wheeled round and threw him from his horse.

When Kei was born back, wounded, to the camp, Gwalchmei the courteous knight said, "No one should presume to disrupt the meditation of a knight, for it may be that he is grieving a loss or thinking of the woman he loves." Then Gwalchmei himself went to the unknown knight, and spoke gently with him.

Peredur said to him: "I did not wish to be disturbed. My thoughts were on the woman of my heart, for I saw in the raven and the snow and the red pearls of blood, her black hair, her eyebrows, the white of her skin and the blush of her cheeks."

"That was a fine meditation," said Gwalchmei. "Nor would a man wish to be taken from it."

The Game of Fidchell

Finn mac Cumhail had two men to carry his *fidchell* board: Gúaire, the "One-eyed," and Flaithius, the "Keen-edged." A Fenian, named Finn Bán, came over to play a game with Gúaire. The wager was three ounces of gold against three days' play. But Finn Bán was one of the four most skilled *fidchell* players, the others being Diarmuid, Flaithius and Finn himself. Thus it was that during the three days Gúaire failed to win a single game and lost his bet. Then he swore at Finn Bán, hurling insults at him and saying he was a poor fighter, having no skill with weapons. At this Finn Bán lashed out and punched Gúaire in the mouth, so that six of his front teeth were knocked out and he collapsed onto the fidchell board. When news of this reached Finn, he demanded the head of Finn Bán in retribution for the blow, but Oisin restrained him. Then this judgement was made: that whenever Finn passed the servant of Finn Bán, he might punch him with his fist.

The Counsel of Finn

Be a peace-maker in the house,
be strong in the wild.
Forbear to strike your hound
or slander your wife without cause.
Keep away from the fool, especially in battle.
Respect the holy man, and avoid dispute.
Shun the woman of dark craft and the evil man.
Show courtesy to women and household servants,
give respect to poets, craftsmen and soldiers.
Offer friends and advisers the best seat.
Do not swear false oaths, or seek to please all men.
Avoid boasting, promise only what you can give,
for a fine promise, if proved empty, is a humiliation.
Be loyal to your lord and patron,
do not betray him for gold or riches.
Avoid complaining speech, lies and impetuous gossip.
Avoid the ale-house, do not consort with the crowd,
take good advice and be kind to the elderly.
Be ever wary, for your enemy may lie near.
Be open-handed with your possessions,
be ready to fight in a good cause,
at all times be hospitable, courteous and open-handed.

The City of Ludd

King Beli the Great had three sons—Ludd, Caswallaun and Nynniaw, the eldest being Ludd. After the death of Beli, Ludd became ruler of the kingdom of Britain. He ruled it well and wisely and the people prospered. He was a model king, brave in battle, generous, and giving freely of his hospitality. He commanded that the walls around his favourite city be rebuilt. When that was done he surrounded it with many fine towers to protect it. Then he commanded the citizens to build grand houses in the city so that no other would rival it. For, of all his many cities and forts, of which he had many, he loved this one the best. He made his main dwelling in it and called it Caer Ludd. Afterwards it was called Caer Lundein and in later times, a new and foreign people called it Londres or Lunden.

The Wisdom of a King

Cormac, the exiled prince, returned to Tara, to the Court of Lugaid, but remained in hiding. He took employment herding sheep for a poor widow. One day one of her sheep broke into the Queen's vegetable garden and ate some of the produce. King Lugaid was very angry and demanded the widow be brought before him. He ordered that the sheep be made forfeit to the Queen in recompense for its crime. At this the herd boy came forward, saying: "The penalty is unjust, O king, if, for the sake of a few vegetables, the poor widow must lose her livelihood."

The King was taken aback: "And what would the wise boy decree instead?" he asked.

"That the sheep's wool be taken for payment since both wool and vegetables have the ability to grow again. Then, after a while, both parties will forget their hurt." At this, the court burst into applause.

Lugaid said in alarm and astonishment: "It is the wisdom of a king."

HOLLY AND OAK

The oak and the holly
when they are both full grown
the oak fights the holly king
on midsummer's morn.

The oak beats the holly king
and reigns for half a year
but the holly rises up again
when winter draws near.

The holly fights the oak king
on midwinter's day
the holly beats the oak king
and bears the crown away.

But when the sun is come again
at the waxing of the year
the oak rises up
for his crowning draws near.

The maiden of the springtime
loves the holly of the field
but the maid of the summer
to the oak tree must yield.

The oak king and the holly king
are joined in a dance
both winter and summer
by the Maiden entranced.

THE HUNTING OF THE WREN

The ancient custom of hunting the wren took place annually on 1 January. It was linked with the idea of sacrificial kingship because the wren was at one time considered the King of the Birds. There was a story which told how the birds once held a contest to see which of them should be King. It was decided that the honour should go to the bird who could fly the highest. All the birds soared into the air, but the eagle rose higher than the others. Just as the eagle thought it had flown high enough to claim the title, a little wren, who had been hiding in its feathers, darted out and fluttered a hand's span above its head. Through its cunning, the wren won the contest and was declared King.

The hunting of the wren is carried out at the darkest time of the year symbolising the ritual sacrifice required of the king, in order that the Sovereignty of the land could select a new mate.

Winter Cold

Cold is the winter,
and the wind is bitter
yet the raging stag bellows
against the mountain.

ORAN'S REVELATION

St Columcille began building a chapel on Iona, but whatever was built by day was overthrown at night. He set men to watch but found them dead next morning, so he decided to watch himself. That night a great creature, half-woman and half-fish came out of the sea. Columcille asked her what was killing his people. She said it was fear of her. Then he asked how he could stop the destruction of the building. She said that a man must be buried alive beneath the foundations. When Columcille told this to the men, his brother Oran offered himself for burial, asking to be placed upright with a roof above his head. After this was done, the building work commenced for twenty days, then Columcille commanded that the grave be opened. Oran leaped from the grave and wherever he looked the fields and rushes turned red. He said:

> Heaven is not as it has been spoken
> nor is Hell as it has been taught
> for the good are not forever happy
> nor are the evil forever sad.

Columcille quickly returned him to his grave so that his revelations might not be heard. But to this day the red tips of the rushes testify to his brief resurrection.

Lament for the Poet Mael Mhuru

The earth has never covered such a one
never have the high-towered walls of Tara
nor Ireland's broad green fields
enfolded such a man as Mach Mhuru.

There is none gentler, none so pure
none who has drained death's cup so bravely,
nor have the shadowed spirits ever welcomed
or the rich earth covered one so rare as he.

THE DEATH OF CUCHULAINN

On his way to battle Cuchulainn saw a woman by the ford weeping and washing bloodstained garments in the stream. When she raised them from the water, he saw they were his. Then he came upon three hags roasting a dog. They offered him meat and he accepted to avoid discourtesy, so breaking his *geis*. After that he went into battle and flung his great spear three times. The first time it went through ten men and was hurled back at him, killing Laeg, his charioteer. The second time he hurled it, it was flung back at his horse, the Grey of Macha. The third time it was caught and flung back at Cuchulainn himself, ripping open his belly. Cuchulainn stumbled to the loch and drank from it. Then he made his way to a pillar-stone and tied his belt around his breast and the pillar-stone so that he would die standing up. Seeing this, some of the warriors gathered round but were afraid to approach because of the hero-light that was on him. But when a raven flew down and alighted on his shoulder, they knew that he was dead.

THE ROCK OF THE WEAPONS

Crosach asked Cailte about the great stone called the Rock of the Weapons. "On this rock," said Cailte, "we of the Fianna used to sharpen our weapons every year at Samhain. Nor did their edges diminish the whole year in our fighting and skirmishes. And also on that rock was the great arm-ring, the peace-token of the land. A hundred and sixty ounces of red gold were used in its making and it was ribbed. It was laid in a special hole in the rock where all might see it. But such was the regard for the kings at that time and for the wisdom of the Druids, that no one dared steal it. But after the last battle, the battle of Gabair, I myself turned the rock over."

Crosach said, "I would like to see the hole that held the arm-band."

Then Cailte stretched his arms around the rock and heaved it up from the earth. When he had done that, he revealed the cleft in it and the ring-band still inside it. Then Cailte broke the ring-band in two halves. He gave one half to St Patrick and the other to the people of those parts.

The Division of the Kingdom

Cailte and Oisin were the last, and most ancient, survivors of the Fianna, being some three hundred years old. One day they were with the King of Ireland. He said to them: "Tell me more about the old Irish kings and the deeds of the Fianna."

Cailte answered, "On this hill, the kingdom of Ireland was divided between the two sons of Feradach, Túathal and Fiacha. The older one took the great feasting halls, the treasures, the herds of sheep and cattle, the gold and silver jewellery, goblets and drinking horns, the forts and manors. The younger one took the rivers and cliffs, the fruit of the sea, the red-flecked salmon, the creatures of the land, the wild stags, red deer and fierce boars."

"The two shares are not equal," said the King's men.

"Ah," said Oisín, "which would you choose? The fine houses, treasures and riches of the land, or the forests and wild places, the hunting and fishing?"

But before they answered, Cailte said, "The share that you think is worse is the one we think is better."

The Three Deadly Smiles

The smile of the snow when beginning to melt,
the smile of a wife who has come from her lover,
the smile of a mastiff hound ready to spring.

SPRING

THE second of the great Celtic lunar festivals was that of Imbolc, sometimes called Oimelc, which took place around 1 February. Its name means "around the belly" and the festival was a celebration of the great Goddess and of new birth. At this time, the Cailleach, or old crone, was renewing and transforming herself into the spring maiden.

Agriculturally, it was the time of first shoots, so early flowers, such as the snowdrop, were dedicated to the Goddess. In the fields newborn lambs were struggling to their feet, a sign of oncoming spring and the re-fertilisation of the earth. Domestically it was a time when women's work reflected the movements of the seasons and the rhythms of nature. Activities such as lighting fires in the hearth, smooring the fires with ashes at night to prevent them going out, milking cows, weaving cloth, preparing food, churning butter, were all acknowledged at this time and related to the Celtic goddess Brighid.

Imbolc

Brighid, whose name means "the exalted one," was the daughter of the Dagda, the "Good God" of the Tuatha de Danann. She was patroness of poetry, healing and smithcraft. As goddess of poetry, she fostered the sacred word—so highly prized by the Druids; as goddess of healing, she was the protecting mother, the bringer of blessings and caster-out of disease and sickness; and as goddess of smithcraft, she was linked to the sacred power of fire, and was sometimes known as the Celtic fire goddess.

Imbolc, therefore, was Brighid's feast, the goddess being the incarnation of the Great Mother as the reborn maiden. Brighid was associated with the colour white because she gifted the earth with the new milk of the ewes and with the first flower, the snowdrop. White, therefore, came to symbolise purity and new birth. The white dress and veil worn at marriage ceremonies, and the "bride" itself, come from this goddess.

The festival of Imbolc was the time of new beginnings, hope, cleansing and healing. Its celebrations involved the lighting of candles and the kindling of fires. Because the weather was not conducive to travel, there was no great gathering place for the festival, instead it was concentrated on the home and was marked by more domestic rituals. For example, a corn effigy of Brighid was carried out of the house, which was then cleaned and made pure by the women. Afterwards the effigy was brought into the house again with great ceremony. For Brighid presided over the hearth, seat of the central fire and flame of the home which gave warmth and heated the cooking pot, thus nurturing the physical body and, on a spiritual level, providing a perpetually burning symbol of divinity.

Besides being the fire goddess, Brighid was also linked with water. She was associated in particular with holy wells and springs because of their healing properties. She was also connected with baptism. Early Celtic rituals of baptism involved both fire and water, the infant being carried clockwise three times round a fire, and then sprinkled with water from a holy well.

The Celtic goddess later became confused with the saintly Abbess born around 450 CE and known as St Bridget, or St Bride. Around 470 Bridget founded a convent in Kildare or Cille Dara—Cell of the Oak, which had originally been the site of a Druidic grove. The Christian Bridget, therefore, had links with Druidry, and was even said to have had a Druid father. Her convent became a famous centre of learning, producing some fine illustrated manuscripts. Because of the association with the goddess, nineteen nuns tended a fire that was kept perpetually burning in St Bridget's honour. The sanctuary was surrounded by bushes, and only women were allowed into it.

There are many legends surrounding St Bridget. In one of them, she asks the King of Leinster for land to build her convent, and says she will take as much as her cloak will cover. When the King agrees, she spreads her cloak on the ground and it miraculously grows until it has covered the whole region. Another legend has her hanging her cloak on the rays of the sun. Many stories grew up around St Bridget linking her with Mary and the Christchild. For example, she was believed to have been the foster-mother of Jesus, and to have blessed him with three drops of pure spring-water. She was also said to have been Mary's midwife, assisting at Christ's birth.

Many of the saint's attributes became attached to the Virgin Mary. For example, St Bridget is said to have worn a crown of candles round her head and her feast-day was celebrated by the lighting of candles. Later, the festival of Candlemas, at which candles were brought into church and blessed, was dedicated to the Virgin Mary. The link between the two women was very strong. Underlying both their stories was the ancient Celtic belief in the virginity of the Spring Goddess and of her role in conceiving the solar king-child who was to be born at the winter solstice.

Throughout the season of spring, that ran from Imbolc to the Festival of Beltain on 1 May, the Celts honoured the Goddess and anticipated her gifts of bounty. The solar festival of the spring equinox, celebrated around 21 March, also falls in this period. This is the time when the sun crosses the equator and when day and night are of equal length. This festival was held on the first day of the full moon after the vernal equinox. It, too, was associated with women, later becoming known as Lady Day. Originally it was held in honour of Eostre, the goddess of fertility. Eggs and white rabbits featured in the celebrations, being the symbols of birth and fertility, and her sacred animal, the hare, was also honoured. At this time, the Great Goddess was believed to descend into the Underworld for three days—the three dark days of the moon, before appearing again. This belief arose from the observation of the agricultural seasonal round, and echoes that of the Greek myth of Persephone, who was abducted by Hades and taken down into the Underworld.

The meditations for this season are concerned with the Maiden aspect of the Goddess, the stirrings of nature, new birth and new beginnings. They include courtship, preparations for summer, and plans for war—spring being the time for the training of warriors. They also include symbolic colours, sacred trees and animals, smithcraft, the prophetic gifts of the seer, the shapeshifting abilities of the shaman, love, fertility, and the element of air.

INVOCATION TO BRIGHID

Brighid of the holy wells,
light-bringer
hope-bearer
comforter to women in labour
and lambs in the cold fields.
Brighid—eternal flame
hidden in heart,
Bring blessings.

Bride,
crowned with candles
cleanser and healer,
pure as snow
milk-white,
golden-haired
guardian of the sacred word,
mystical flame-bearer,
inspirer of women.

THE SACRED ELEMENT OF AIR

Sacred element of air, invisible realm of spirit, Breath of Life. Enlightening one, resonant with sound of speech and music, mystic carrier of perfume and the smoke of incense. Transporter of thought and quickening agent of imagination. Bearer of the Sacred Word, the highest magic. Dimension of winds, the fourfold messengers. Dome of the sun, the sky, the heavens, and all celestial splendour. Winged ones hover on your breezes, the Tuatha ride as mist upon you, druids conjure with their wands your airy powers. Refining spirit, all-pervading, whispering the secrets of the soul. Weightless are you, transparent, pure. Flights of inspiration rise in you, flashes of insight shoot through you like lightning, meditation lifts the spirit to your open spaces, the power of thought is rarified within you. Limitless one, bestowing freedom; flame and moisture vanish in your endless empire. East is your direction, realm of dawn and the awakening sun. New beginnings, strength and wonder are your properties, element of joy and highest understanding.

THE SWORD OF NUADA

Sword of Nuada of the Silver Hand,
You came with the mist that carried the Tuatha,
Sharp blade of intellect and breath of life,
East is illumination and the rising light.

When the Tuatha de Danann brought their four mystical gifts to Ireland, the second gift, and the one linked with the direction of the East and with the element of air, was the Sword of Nuada. Nuada was a Celtic king who at one time lost an arm in battle. This required him to step down from kingship, as it was a rule among the Celts that a blemished king could not reign over them. However, when a silver hand was made for him by Diancecht the physician, he was allowed to resume his kingship. The property of Nuada's magic sword was such that whoever brandished it was rendered invincible.

The power of the sword in Celtic understanding was linked with the wielding of justice; it was the symbol of kingship and chief weapon of the warrior. Being connected with the element of air, it also denoted truth, reason and the power of the word. Like the tongue, it could be double-edged. A masculine symbol, the sword-blade was often described as glittering, being also connected with light and the rays of the sun. The scabbard was considered to have healing properties, as in the case of Arthur's sword, Excalibur.

CORMAC MAC ART
AND THE SILVER BRANCH

Cormac, the High King of Tara, looked out from his window one morning and saw a young man standing on the green holding in his hand a silver faerie branch with three golden apples upon it. When he shook the branch it produced the most magical and delightful music that had ever been heard in the land. Added to this, whoever heard it, whether they were in pain, sickness or sorrow of heart, immediately forgot their trouble and were lulled into a soothing sleep. Cormac went to meet the youth and asked to make an alliance with him. Then he asked for the silver branch. "You can have it," replied the youth, "if you grant me three requests." Cormac agreed, so the youth gave him the branch and went on his way. A year later he returned to claim his price. The three requests he demanded of Cormac were his daughter, his son and his wife. Each in turn were compelled to go with the youth, to the sorrow and despair of the King and all his citizens.

Cuchulainn's Training
in Arms and Love

When Cuchulainn was of age to be trained in arms, he was sent to Scathach, a woman who lived on an island in Alba and who was considered the finest warrior in the land. When he drew near to her island, he encountered the Pupil's Bridge which was impossible to cross, for as soon as any weight was laid upon it, it would tip up. Three times Cuchulainn attempted the bridge and three times he was thrown back, but the fourth time he made his hero's Salmon Leap, which took him right across the bridge and onto the island. Then he banged on Scathach's gate with the point of his spear, piercing through the wood. Scathach's daughter Uathach came to meet him and immediately conceived a great desire for him.

After Cuchulainn had proved himself in combat with Scathach's champion, he held the point of his sword to her chest and asked her to grant him three requests. "You may have them if you can state them in one breath," she replied. So Cuchulainn asked her to give him full training in arms, her daughter for his bed, and to prophesy his future, for Scathach was also a seer. These three requests were granted to him.

FROECH IN THE DARK POOL

When Findabhair saw Froech swimming in the dark pool she said:

> Nothing is more beautiful than Froech in the dark pool
> his body white as snow, his streaming hair,
> his well-proportioned face, his deep blue eyes,
> a perfect youth, unblemished and straight-limbed,
> carrying on his back a branch of ash;
> a spray, red-berried,
> lies between his face and his white throat.

SYMBOLIC COLOURS—WHITE

White was used extensively in Celtic poetry in descriptions of untouched snow, shining teeth, magical animals, spring flowers and linen garments. Most of all it was used to symbolise the purity and beauty of a lover's skin, whether man or woman. In the description of the beautiful young man Froech, who is bathing in a pool, attention is drawn to his unblemished white body. The description of his white skin was linked to the Celtic reverence for purity symbolised by bodily perfection. No Celtic king could reign if he had any blemish on him.

White being the colour of purity, it also symbolised spirituality. White horses, deer and hounds were usually connected with the Otherworld. Faerie women such as Rhiannon and Niamh rode white horses, white harts led unwary hunters such as Pwyll into Otherworldly realms, and the hounds of Annwn were described as white-haired with red-tipped ears. White was a threshold colour that led between the material and spiritual worlds. The Druids wore white robes, and white bulls were involved in the sacred ceremony of culling the mistletoe from the sacred oak grove. White was also associated with the goddess Brighid, who was linked with the snowdrop, first flower of the spring, and virgin purity.

THE ORDER OF OVATE

The second Druidic order, after the bardic training had been completed, was that of the Ovate. This higher order penetrated further into the realms of the unknown and involved training in techniques of inspirational knowledge and prophecy. "The Ovates," wrote the Roman writer Ammianus, "investigated the sublime and attempted to explain the secret laws of nature." The Ovates were poet-seers, called *filidh*, in Ireland, and besides being skilled in divination, they were also herbalists and healers. They also had shamanic powers, becoming shapeshifters and in this way entering the animal and spirit worlds in order to receive special knowledge. One of their responsibilities was to gather information from the close observation of nature. Their methods of divination included interpreting the stars and planets, the flight of birds, the shape of clouds, and the meaning of dreams. They also conjured prophetic visions, practised augury through touch, and received inspirational knowledge by composing poetry. Their chief responsibility was to keep the Celtic people in touch with the truths of the Otherworld and to maintain harmony between the worlds.

THE THREE DIVINATORY PRACTICES

In exercising their prophetic powers, the Ovates used three distinct divinatory practices. The first was *imbas forosna*—divination through dream. To obtain this they chewed the flesh of an animal, such as a pig, bull, dog or cat, spoke an invocation over the chewed meat and called on the spirits for guidance. Then, attended by *awen,* or watchers, they fell into a sleep during which they would be given a dream containing a message for the whole tribe. The second form of divination was *teinm laeghda*—revelation by means of poetic inspiration. In this, the truth would appear to them as they composed a poem on the subject in question. The third was *dichetul do chennaib*, divination through the finger-ends. Using this method, when they touched a person or object with their wand or fingers, they could divine its history. These, then, were the three divinatory skills that belonged to the Ovates: the dreaming vision, the inspirational vision and the vision that comes by touch.

HAZEL—THE POET'S TREE

Called *coll* or *cuill*, the hazel was perhaps the most magical of Celtic trees. Helmeted with leafy frills, its nuts were believed to contain the essence of poetic inspiration. Nine sacred hazel trees surrounded the "Well of Wisdom" where the famous Salmon of Wisdom lurked who would eat their reddish fruits and imbibe Otherworldly knowledge. Linked to the element of air, hazel wands were used by druids to conjure magical and inspirational power from the Otherworld. Hazel was also linked to water and used for dowsing. Its catkins resemble lambs' tails and often appear in January, heralding an early spring. At Beltain burning wands of hazel were used to singe the hides of cattle in order to ward off elemental spirits. In the *Dindsenchas*, the Law Tracts of Ireland, felling the hazel carried the death penalty.

> *Coll*, Bringer of Wisdom
> light, airy one,
> bright-branched rod of inspiration,
> swifter than thought
> you shoot out intuition.
> Your lithe brown wands
> touch powers unseen.
> Fleet, magical,
> the hands of druids
> dance your ecstasies.

THE TRICKSTER

The figure of the trickster lies somewhere between the fool and the magician. The Ovate or shaman demonstrates the power of the trickster in his magical powers and his ability to shapechange. The trickster is bold and mischievous and enjoys playing with elements of the Otherworld. The irrational, the inventive, the unexpected are his tools. He is master of disguises and the power of illusion. He can perceive the reality behind appearance which gives him an innate wisdom. Cunning is one of his characteristics and his trickster qualities can be put to good or bad use. Yet his flexibility, his fearlessness and the knowledge he acquires through play are vital qualities that need to be called upon at times of testing or initiation. The king in Celtic myth was often accompanied by a magician or jester who provided a link with unruly forces which, in wise hands, could become agents of flexibility, change and innovation.

THE INNER WOLF OR *FAOL*

The wolf represents wildness but also strength and faithfulness. It is fearless and intuitive and was greatly respected by the Celts. In fact, the Celts crossed wolves with hounds in order to produce fighting dogs for battle. The wolf was considered intelligent and even companionable, often becoming the friend of hermits and other holy men living alone in the forest. A daring ally, the wolf symbolises inner power, and can lead the way into unfamiliar territory, break down barriers and release new energies. A social animal, it is able to adapt to the pack and yet keep its fierceness. In Irish myth, the Morrigan shapechanges into a wolf to attack Cuchulainn after he spurns her love. In Welsh myth, the magician Gwydion and his brother Gilvaethwy are turned into wolves by King Math as part of their punishment or initiation. Understanding wolf-energy was regarded as particularly valuable in shamanic experience.

SHAPESHIFTING

The training of the Ovate involved the use of shamanic power. This was the power to shapeshift into animals. The Ovate might achieve this by means of ecstatic trance, entering into an animal form in order to commune with its spirit and take on an aspect of its function and knowledge. Ancient cave paintings point to this practice as they are often found in the deepest and most inaccessible caves, suggesting that the shaman went to this depth in order to carry out this difficult and dangerous task undisturbed. Some of the great bards also speak of experiencing different transformations. In his poems, Taliesin claims to have shared the knowledge of animals and birds, and even of inanimate objects and elements of nature such as a shield, a harpstring, a wave and a star. The wizard Gwydion was also a shapeshifter and under the tutelage of Math was turned first into a deer, then a wolf and then a sow. Shamans often wore feathered cloaks to symbolise their affinity with the natural world.

Deep in the forest
I crouch.
Wolf-weird comes on me
wind-swift blur of trees
snap at fox-tail,
fangs blood-drip,
eyes are moon's
black disc
white-rimmed.
Wild howl,
breath streaking
bracken-soft,
pad-footed,
silent,
ware.

THE BEGETTING OF AENGUS OG

In the days of the most ancient gods, the Dagda, known as the Good God, or Many-skilled, conceived a passion for the woman Boann. This woman lived on the River Boyne with her husband Elcmar, a powerful chief. The Dagda wished to enjoy her favours without alerting her husband. He therefore made a spell so that Elcmar would mistake a full nine months for a single day. Then the Dagda went to Boann and slept with her.

When nine months were passed she gave birth to Aengus, named Mac in da Og, which means "made in a day." Aengus Og became the God of Love and later tricked Elcmar into giving him kingship of Newgrange, the neolithic passage tomb on the banks of the Boyne, by asking to be allowed to stay there for a day and a night. After Elcmar granted his request, Aengus refused to leave on the grounds that "it is in days and nights that the world passes." When the matter was referred to the Dagda for judgement he found in favour of his son.

SACRED SYMBOLS—THE CIRCLE

In Celtic belief, the circle symbolised the wheel of life. Nothing was fixed or static, everything was in continual ebb and flow. They saw life as being circular rather than linear because they believed in the perpetual renewal of all things. Life gave way to death, which in turn engendered new life. This concept came from the round of the seasons in which the death of nature was endlessly followed by its rebirth. The Goddess, too, turned through her various aspects and transformations in harmony with the seasons. Such circular motion had no beginning or end. It therefore represented universal time, limitlessness, the infinite and eternity. Because of this it was also the symbol of the spirit, the realm of the transcendent, and denoted perfection and completeness. The symbol of the circle was also linked with the sun and with masculine deity. A circle within a square represents the divine spirit contained in matter.

THE BIRTH OF TALIESIN

After Gwion Bach had licked his burning thumb and the three drops of knowledge, wisdom and inspiration had entered him, he fled from the witch Ceridwen using his new powers.

First he changed into a hare
racing across field and farm,
but she became a greyhound
and pounded after him.

He changed into a fish
and swam beneath the foam,
but she became an otter
and dived in after him.

He changed into a bird
and soared up in the air,
but she became a keen-eyed hawk
and swooped upon him there.

He fell down as a tiny grain
among a heap of wheat,
but she became a pecking hen
and took him in her beak.

Nine months later Ceridwen gave birth to a son whose face shone so brightly that she was afraid to kill him. So she wrapped him in a leather pouch and let him ride upon the river to meet his fate. But the boy that she set on the water survived to become the great bard of Wales, known as Taliesin of the Shining Brow.

THE MAGIC OF SMITHCRAFT

The craft of moulding iron into weapons and agricultural implements was considered a magical art by the Celts. The blacksmith used at least twenty different tools which have been excavated at ancient sites. In Irish myth Goibniu is the blacksmith of the Tuatha de Danann. The magic swords and spearheads he forges for the battle of Mag Tuiread deal wounds from which the victim can never recover. Gofannon is his Welsh counterpart, the divine smith alluded to in the *Mabinogion*. He was honoured by being offered the first drink at a feast. Magical weapons such as the Sword of Nuada and the Spear of Lugh, played a key part in Celtic myth. In order to be effective, the spear forged to kill Lleu Llaw Gyffes could only be fashioned on holy days. The great goddess Brighid was patroness of smithcraft as well as poetry, inspiration and healing. Smithcraft was considered a divine art and the blacksmith was a type of mage, dealing in works of transformation and using the element of fire to wield his magic.

ASPECTS OF THE GODDESS THE MAIDEN

Every spring the Goddess of the Land renews herself, becoming a virgin and maiden once more. In this aspect, she represents the epitome of all beauty and desire. It is the Spring Maiden who has the power to lay a *geis* on her consort and lure away her new lover. This ancient seasonal ritual is reflected throughout Celtic mythology. Grainne is such a maiden, choosing Diarmuid, the fairest warrior of the Fenians, as is Deirdre when she commands the warrior Naoise to elope with her. The hand of the maiden is annually contested, the older champion having to yield to the younger one. In this way the continuing health and fertility of the land is ensured.

In the Welsh story of *Math*, Blodeuwedd is a type of the maiden, being created out of leaves, bark and flowers. In Arthurian legend, Guinevere is also such a flowerbride, being fought over by Lancelot, the strongest knight, and abducted by Melvas, King of the Summerlands. When Arianrhod insists on her virginity in the story of Math, she is speaking in terms of the Virgin aspect of the Goddess, of which King Math seems unaware.

ARIANRHOD—THE VIRGIN GODDESS

The silvery stars
wheel about my head,
my palace of Caer Sidi
turns as I turn.
Virgin am I,
mother, crone.

In my tower
is *awen*,
seat of power.
Poets, seers
journey here.

Round my throne
three fiery rings,
in my courtyard
fountains spring.

My light step
silences, my breath
withholds
men's dreams,
for I am
Arianrhod,
Goddess
Virgin
Queen.

THE THREE TESTS OF ARIANRHOD

These three tests I lay on my son, for I am the hard one, the Challenger. And my first test is this: that I will never give him name. And the second is this: that I will never give him arms. And the third is this: that I will never give him leave to marry mortal woman. And now let him do what he must with these three tests from his mother. First let him find out his name by his own skill. Then let him earn his arms by show of courage. And thirdly, being denied mortal woman, let him have the Goddess of the Land for wife. But after he has passed these tests let him die on the World Tree and after, be revived. And do not forget that it was I, Arianrhod, who set his testing and I, Arianrhod who understood his fate. For I am his Mother and his Challenger.

THE SACRED COW

Milk-yielding, benign, nurturing, the cow is an emblem of the goddess in her maternal aspect. It is a creature of the earth, its crescent-shaped horns reflecting the feminine powers of the moon and the horn of plenty. It therefore also signifies nurturing and abundance. Anciently, three sacred cows came out of the sea and appeared on the shores of Ireland. Being white, red and black in colour, they were taken to represent the three aspects of the Great Mother—virgin, mother and crone. The goddess Boann, of the River Boyne, takes her name from *Bo*, meaning cow. Cows were also sacred to the Goddess Brighid who was said to have been raised on the milk of an Otherworldly cow. She was revered as the goddess of cattle and agriculture. The power of the cow could protect against evil. Being intimately connected with the land and agriculture, cattle featured prominently in the great Celtic festivals. At Imbolc, the time of calving was celebrated, and at Beltain, cattle were made to pass between two fires for purification.

Silver Birch—the Lady Tree

Called *beith*, *bith* or *beth*, which means "shining one," the birch is light and airy, a very feminine tree. Not numbered among the chieftain trees in the Druidic calendar, it was nevertheless considered very important. Because of its silver bark it was connected with the land of faerie and because of its being lightly rooted but pliable it symbolised resilience and adaptability. Lovers lingered in its groves at Beltain. Witches' broomsticks were traditionally made from it, and its rods were used magically to clear away negative energies. It was associated with purification and with the element of air. It is one of the earliest trees to come into leaf and denotes fresh beginnings and new birth.

Lady of the Woods,
Beith, Shining-One,
Your silver-coated branches
catch the moon,
your pliant dancing body
plays the sun.
Light-hearted lovers
linger in your groves,
while through your flickering leaves
your shining faerie form inspires
and purifies. You speak
of new beginnings, birth
and cleansing. On your boughs
the hovering spirits fly,
and with your branches
sweep the star-spread sky.

Spring Equinox Solstice

21 March

Time of perfect balance, day with night and light with darkness. Earth reveals new riches, while the Sun-god hangs, waiting to triumph over darkness, waiting to mount the skies towards midsummer. Festival of waxing strength and potency. Time of the Maiden, Virgin Goddess, Lady Day. Feast of beginnings, of Eostre, she of jewelled eggs, spring rabbits, hares, fertility. Goddess disappearing with moon's blackness, deity descending three-days into darkness and the realm of faded spirits. Light-restoring newborn one, quencher of the land of shadows. You who overcome the darkness, ending the grip of coldness, clothing the bare-branched trees, and greening the barren landscape. Hail to you, ice-breaker of the frozen lakes and waters. Hail to you, fair source of springs and gushing rivers. Hail to you, transformer of the power of death and Winter. Hail triumphant herald of the Sun-god's gladness.

THE BINDING POWER OF THE GEIS

The placing of a *geis*, a bond or prohibition, on a hero plays a strong part in Celtic myth. Grainne places one on Diarmuid, forcing him to elope with her. It seems he is bound by the geis more strongly than by his ties of loyalty to Finn, his captain. One text describes Grainne's power of geis as "spells that go with me," which suggests that the geis was more than just a bond of honour, but had a magical element to it. In the same way, Deirdre places a geis on Naoise which compels him to take her for wife.

Besides the prohibitions that are laid on them later in life, heroes are born with certain *geasa* already in place. These seem to be inextricably linked with their fate because breaking them usually heralds their death. Often, too, these geasa are linked with totem animals. For example, Cuchulainn is forbidden to eat dog-meat and only does so shortly before he dies, and Diarmuid, who is forbidden to hunt boar, receives his death wound when he breaks his geis by hunting the Boar of Ben Bulben.

OLWEN

In the story of "Culhwch and Olwen" from the *Mabinogion*, when seeking the hand of Olwen, Culhwch has to undergo a list of tasks imposed on him by Olwen's father, the Giant Ysbaddaden. In order to accomplish these tasks, he takes a band of warriors with him including King Arthur. Although he knows of Olwen's beauty only by hearsay, when she first appears she surpasses all expectation. Like Blodeuwedd, Olwen is a type of flowerbride. She has obvious goddess qualities and is intimately connected with nature and the land.

… then Olwen entered
   like a slender dancing flame in crimson silk,
   a heavy golden torc about her neck,
   gem-studded. Brighter than sunlight
   was her hair and yellower than the blossom of the broom.
   Whiter than sparkling foam her skin,
   her palms and fingers delicate as petalled melilot
   that grows by running springs. Her eyes
   were fairer than hawk or gentle falcon, her two breasts
   were purer white than swans' down, her red lips,
   softer and deeper-hued than foxgloves. As she came
   the heart of each one watching leaped
   towards her. Where she walked
   she left white footprints, trefoils,
   clover flowers.

Arthur at the Battle of Bath

Arthur wore a leather jerkin, a gold helmet with a dragon-shaped crest and, across his shoulders, Pridwen, his circular shield, emblazened with the image of the Virgin Mary. From his belt hung Caliburn, his invincible sword, and in his hand was his great spear, Ron. He drew up his men and prepared to attack the Saxons. All day they fought and the Saxons had the better of them, being greater in number. The next day they fared much the same until Arthur, realising that his side lacked any hope of victory, suddenly went berserk. Drawing his sword, he called on the name of the blessed Virgin and rushed at the thickest part of the enemy, striking out and calling on God with each stroke. In this way he killed each man outright with a single blow. Nor did he slacken his onslaught until four hundred and seventy men were killed by his hand. Seeing this, the Britons poured after him, dealing death as they came. Such was the onslaught led by Arthur that he gained the upper hand and the Saxons turned and fled.

ARTHUR AND GWLADYS

Arthur was playing dice on a hilltop near the River Severn with his companions Kei and Bedwyr when a horse came into view, pounding along at full speed. On it were a young man and a beautiful woman. Arthur sent his companions to enquire after their trouble. They reported back that the King of Glamorgan was eloping with his love, Gwladys, because her father would not give his consent to their union. But Gwladys was so stately and beautiful that Arthur immediately conceived a great desire for her. So strong was his lust, that he commanded Kei and Bedwyr to seize her and bring her to him. Appalled, they replied: "Are you not ashamed of such bad thoughts. Have you forgotten that we are supposed to help others and not do violence to them!" After their admonitions, Arthur reluctantly offered to help the fleeing couple and aid their escape.

THE ISLAND OF ALBION

Albion, fairest of islands
in length eight hundred miles
in breadth two hundred.
Providing in plenty everything
men could want. Rich stores
of minerals, wide plains
and sloping hills for bearing crops.
Forests, well-stocked
with different kinds of game.
Woodland glades and pastures,
waving corn, and grass for feeding cattle.
Many-coloured flowers, refreshing blooms
offering their pollen to the worrying bees.
Wind-swept mountains, grassy meadows,
deep, transparent springs and streamlets,
speaking their sleepy murmurs.
Rivers rich with fish—three noblest ones
the Thames, the Humber and the Severn,
stretching their arms in welcome
to the ocean's bravest vessels
bringing their merchandise from overseas,
enriching this beauteous land.

THE WONDROUS CITY OF YS

Dahut, the mermaid's child, came to her father, King Gradlon, and implored him to help her. The King was shocked to see how thin and pale his beautiful daughter had become and he promised with tears in his eyes, to do anything he could for her.

"Then build me a city upon the water," she said, "a wondrous city that hangs above the waves, a city with high white towers and golden cupolas that shimmer to their reflections, a city where there is joy and dance and feasting, a city of fountains and courtyards, of broad walks and wide avenues, a city that will be famed throughout the world for its riches and its splendour."

So Gradlon commanded the best builders, goldsmiths, workers of art and craftmanship in the land, and soon the wondrous city of Ys rose up upon the Pointe du Raz, that westerly rocky promontory, like a fair bride in gold-rayed magnificence. And after it was built the fame of the city travelled far and wide, as did the fame of the beauty of the princess who held court in it.

SACRED NUMBERS—FOUR

The number four symbolises material life. It is the sacred number of earth and of the manifest world. The Celts believed the world was formed from the four elements, earth, fire, air and water. These in turn corresponded to the four directions and to the four seasons. When the faerie race, the Tuatha de Danann, first overcame Ireland, they brought with them the Four Sacred Gifts which corresponded to the four elements, namely, the *Lia Fail*, or Stone of Destiny, the fiery Spear of Lugh, the Sword of Nuada, and the Cauldron of the Dagda. The symbolism of these four hallowed objects permeated Celtic belief and mythology. Later they became part of medieval and Arthurian legend, the sword in the stone denoting mystical kingship and the lance and the cup reappearing in the Quest of the Holy Grail. Today the power of four survives in the four suits of playing cards and in the Minor Arcana of coins, wands, spears and cups found in the Tarot.

How Aengus Won Caer

Aengus, the god of love, was visited in his dreams every night by a lovely maiden. He pined for her for a year. Then Boann, his mother, seeing he was so pale and wan, sent men out to seek her. They searched in vain until one day, Aengus' father, the Dagda, found her in the realm of faerie. Her name was Caer and she was held by a great enchantment, taking the shape of a swan every other year. Undeterred, Aengus set himself to win her. He came to a lake and saw one hundred and fifty white swans swimming on it with chains of silver around their necks and tongues of gold on top of their heads. He stood close to the edge of the water and called the swan to him, "Caer," he cried, "speak to me Caer. It is I, Aengus." She came to him and he threw his arms around her. Then he took the form of a swan himself and they fell asleep together. On waking, they rose into the air and circled the lake three times and flew off to Bruigh Maic, singing a song of such power it caused all who heard it to fall asleep for three days and nights.

SONG OF AMERGIN

When the Milesians first set foot in Ireland, their chief druid Amergin bent himself and blessed the earth. Then he rose up and spoke these words:

> I am the wind blowing over the ocean,
> I am a wave of the sea,
> I am the murmur of the billows,
> I am the ox of seven battles,
> I am the hawk on the crag,
> I am a golden drop of the sun
> I am the fairest of blooms,
> I am a wild boar in boast
> I am a salmon in the pool,
> I am a lake on the plain,
> I am the craft of the poet,
> I am the word of knowledge,
> I am the spearpoint of battle,
> I am the inspirer of man with the fire of thought.
> I, alone, know the secret of the stone door.

AMERGIN GIVES THE THREE NAMES OF POWER TO IRELAND

After speaking his sacred words on the land, Amergin told his men to go forward over the land and bestow on it Three Names of Power in order to secure it for ever. As they travelled, a woman came to them in great grief saying she was a dishonoured queen who had been stripped of all her possessions.

"What is your name?" asked Amergin.

"Banba," said the woman.

"Then," said Amergin, "I shall put your name upon the land. Banba, it shall be called." And this was the Giving of the First Name.

After that a second woman came to them. She was proud and warrior-like and lamented that she no longer had a chariot to carry her for she too had been dishonoured. Then Amergin said the land would be named Fodhla after her. And this was the Giving of the Second Name.

A third woman then approached in the shape of an old crone, weeping and sighing at her lot and said she had once been a great queen but was now bowed low. Amergin said that the land should be named Erin after her. And this was the Giving of the Third Name.

Thus the land was given to the three queens, Banba, Fodhla and Erin, who became the triple Sovereignty of Ireland.

THE DISASTROUS PILLOWTALK

In the royal bed lay Medbh, Queen of Connaught, and her husband Ailill. It was Ailill who made the first dangerous comment: "It is good for a wife to have a wealthy husband," he said.

"Yes, indeed," replied Medbh, "But why do you say that?"

"I was thinking how much better off you are now than when you first married me."

"I was perfectly well off before then!" she retorted.

"That is news to me," said Ailill, "I only know about the woman's things you brought with you."

"On the contrary, my father gave me a whole province of Ireland. So, if it comes to riches, why—you are a kept man, for my fortune is greater than yours."

"How can you say that? I have more wealth and property than anyone!"

Then all their possessions were brought out and counted, from the lowliest pots to the costliest clothes and jewels. Their herds of sheep and cattle were counted, their horses, rams and boars, and it was found that in all things their properties matched equally, with one exception: Ailill had a fine bull, Finnbennach the White-horned, and Medbh had no bull to match him. Then Medbh sent to find if in the whole of Ireland any bull might be found the equal of the White-horned.

THE PERCEPTIVENESS OF THE HAWK

The hawk, *seabhac* in Irish, and *gwalch* in Welsh, has been connected with hunting from ancient times. A noble bird, it is far-sighted and proud and linked with chivalry. It is also powerful and dangerous and symbolic of the sun, because it flies so high. Arthur's chief knight was called Gwalchmei, "Hawk of May," who later became known as Gawain. Gwalchmei was the model of chivalric courtesy and was also connected with the sun, his strength waxing at midday, and waning thereafter. In Irish myth, the Hawk of Achill tells Fintan, the ancient shapechanging seer, about its life.

> I am the Hawk of Achill
> keen-eyed, grey-feathered.
> Each night I make my feast
> on fish or venison. Wild flesh
> I tear with my beak, my claws
> hold my prey. I swoop
> across waters, chasms and
> mountain-tops. Harsh is my
> song, my wings rise,
> the bellied wind
> holds them
> while I beat
> into the sun's
> bright
> face.

THE MAGIC PIGS

The pig was a powerful totem animal for the Celts. It was highly magical and was connected with the Underworld. In the Welsh myth of Math from the *Mabinogion*, Pryderi's much-prized pigs were a gift from Arawn, King of the Underworld. There is also the Irish tale of the elusive pigs of Cruachu. It was said that when they came out of the magic cave of Cruachu, the gateway to the Underworld, any place where they stopped became barren for seven years afterwards. Also, if anyone attempted to count their number they would immediately depart to another land. Because of this they were never fully counted. "There are three," one would say. "No, seven," would say another. "I see eleven," "No, thirteen!" Once when Queen Medbh and her husband Ailill tried to count them, one jumped over Medbh's chariot. "O, that is an extra one," she cried and tried to catch it. But it slipped away leaving its hide in her hand, so that no one, not even Medbh, could find out their number.

THE BRAIN-BALL OF CONFLICT AND THE PRIDE OF A KING

If an Ulsterman killed a warrior in single combat he would extract his brains and mix them with lime to make a hard ball. The balls were kept and brought out during disputes. One day Cet came to Ulster looking for mischief. He snatched the brain of Meis-Geghra from two men who were playing with it and hung it from his belt. Then he waited for an opportunity to use it. Not long after, he caused a skirmish between some Ulster and Connaught men, and King Conchobor joined in the fight. When the king appeared, the women of Connaught asked him to come over so that they could admire him, for Conchobor was at that time the fairest man in Ireland—in proportion of figure, in his features, in courtesy, wisdom, dress and bearing, there was none to rival him. Flattered, Conchobor came to the women, but Cet was hiding among them. Cet fitted the brain-ball into a sling and shot it at Conchobor. It entered his skull, and Conchobor's physician said he would die if the ball were removed. So the ball remained in him, but after that time he could not exert himself in any way for fear of bringing on his death.

THE CAVE OF CRUACHU AND
THE SHE-WOLVES

From that same cave of Cruachu which contained the magic pigs came three she-wolves that troubled the land each year, killing the sheep. This was told to Cailte by his friend Cas Corach, who asked if he had a remedy for it. Cailte said that the three wolves were the three daughters of Airitech. "If they can be persuaded to come in human form they can be killed."

"How can they be made to do that?" he asked.

"They would come for men playing harps or lutes," said Cailte.

Then Cas Corach took his lute and went to the top of the cairn and played from early morning until evening until he saw the she-wolves come to him. They laid down and listened to his music and after that they went into the cave again.

"Go back tomorrow," said Cailte.

So, at Cailte's instruction, Cas Corach went back the next day and drew them out again with his music. This time he said to them, "If you could take on human form, the music would be even sweeter to your ears." In this way he charmed the dark skins from them, for they peeled them off so that they were in human form listening to the plaintive faerie music. While they listened, Cailte crept up and sent his deadly spear through all three of them. So the glen where they met their death was known as the Glen of the Werewolves from that day.

SONG OF THE BLACKBIRD (1)

From your nest in the hedge
little blackbird, go well.
Melodious and tranquil is your voice
unlike the hermit's harsh bell.

SONG OF THE BLACKBIRD (2)

From the point of your yellow beak
comes a whistling call,
blackbird on the yellow sprouting branch
sending song over the waters of Loch Loích.

THE HERMIT AND THE FISH

Gradlon, King of Cornouaille in Brittany, was out hunting with his men in the Forest of Menez-Hom when night fell and they needed shelter. They came upon a lonely hut inhabited by a hermit called Corentin, who offered them hospitality. The hermit went to a nearby well from which he caught a fish. Slicing the fish in two, he threw half back into the well, taking the other half back to his hut. But the half that was returned to the water immediately became whole again, while the half that he cooked for the men, to their astonishment, provided an ample feast.

After they had eaten, Gradlon, marvelling at these miracles, begged the hermit to return with him to his palace in Quimper, offering to make him Bishop. Although reluctant to leave his hermitage in the woods, Corentin at last consented. During the years after he came to the palace, he encouraged Gradlon to build churches throughout the land. But as the churches rose up, Dahut, the King's daughter, began to sicken, and it seemed that there was no way in which she could regain her health.

THE HERMIT'S SONG

Dear to me is my little hut in the woods
Where pine-nuts and berries are my food
And the sweet well-water which refreshes me.

Sad would I be to leave my brothers the trees
For to me they are a living temple to my God
Which the wind makes to speak his praise continually.

Dear to me also are my little brothers the birds
Who daily sing their offices at dawn and dusk,
And the woodland creatures who keep vigil with me.

Sad would I be to leave the herbs and plants and grasses
That have been my strength and salve in times of weakness,
And the living streams that tongue the praises of my God.

Dear to me is my little brother the fish
Who joyously jumps from the well to feed me
And nourishes body and soul with his wisdom.

THE TRAINING OF THE FIANNA

The tests of the warrior who wished to join the Fianna were of a very high order. First he was required to know the Twelve Books of Poetry and have mastered the art of poetic composition. Next he must endure being buried waist-deep in earth and defend himself with a shield and a hazel stick while nine warriors cast spears at him—and in this he was not to suffer any wounding. After that his hair was braided and he was chased through the forest. If any warrior overtook him, or if he cracked a stick underfoot or if even a braid of his hair was disturbed during the test then he forfeited the right to join the Fianna. Added to this he had to leap over a branch set at head height, run at full speed at knee-height and extract a thorn from his foot without slackening speed. When he had passed all these tests he was accepted into the Fianna but was not permitted to take a dowry when he married. By such tests the high skills and nobility of the Irish hero was ensured.

FINN'S TREASURE

Cailte asked the men of Conall to help him move a great rock embedded in the wall of the fort. The host took one side and Cailte the other, but they were unable to shift it. Then Cailte called Donn. "Here," he said, "you are the son of a great champion and warrior. If between us we move it and treasure is found underneath, you shall have a third of it."

So, using all their strength, the two men heaved at the rock until at last they managed to move it aside. A pit was discovered beneath it, which contained three vats of treasure. One was brimming with gold, another with silver, and the third with costly goblets and drinking horns. Also in the pit was "the Greyish Wand," the great sword of Finn mac Cumhail. Beside this was Finn's pitcher. This was inlaid with one hundred and fifty ounces of gold, one hundred and fifty ounces of silver and one hundred and fifty precious jewels. When all the men had helped themselves to the treasure from the vats, Cailte ordered that Finn's pitcher be given to St Patrick, and his sword, "the Greyish Wand," be presented to the King of Ireland.

THE GENEROSITY OF FINN

If the leaves that the wood lets fall
were made of gold,
if the white waves that lap the shore
were tipped in silver,
Finn would have given it all away.

FINN'S TREASURES ARE PRESENTED TO PATRICK AND THE KING

When Conall presented the golden pitcher to Diarmait, King of Ireland, he gazed on it and said:

"I have never seen a pitcher more magnificent than this. Who did it belong to?"

"My father, Finn mac Cumhail," replied Oisin. "But whoever found this treasure must have found another beside it, the greatest treasure in the whole of Ireland and Scotland."

"If you mean Finn's sword, the 'Greyish Wand,' I have it here," said Conall, and he asked Donn to present it to the King.

When Donn put his hand to the hilt, he found it fitted easily into his palm. Seeing this, Oisin exclaimed, "How is it that you can wield the sword so easily, when only a descendant of Baiscne or Morna should have this ability?"

"Who are you?" asked the King.

"I am the great-grandson of Morna," answered the boy.

Then Oisin said: "Although your father and grandfather were enemies of the Fianna, they were noble men, and so you are dear to us."

Then Donn presented Finn's sword to the King, and asked him for a reward.

"What would you like?" asked the King

"The leadership of the Fianna," the boy replied.

MAELDUN AND THE ISLAND OF REFRESHMENT

On their voyage Maeldun and his men came to an island divided by four walls. The walls were made of very costly materials. One was gold, one silver, the third copper and the fourth crystal. In each division they saw people of noble bearing. In the first were kings, in the second, queens, while the third was full of youths and the fourth was filled with young maidens. The men decided to land on this island and as they reached the shore one of the maidens came towards them and led them into a house. Then she offered them food which she served from a little pot. The food looked like soft cheese, but when they put it in their mouths each man discovered he had on his tongue the taste of the food which pleased him best.

After eating their fill, the men lay down and were overcome by a deep, intoxicating sleep which lasted for three days and nights. When they awoke, they found they were back on their boat, and there was no longer any sign of the maiden or the magical island.

Cuchulainn Woos Emer

Cuchulainn went to the Gardens of Lugh to woo Emer. He found her on the green. She raised her beautiful face and smiled.

"May the road you travel be blessed!" she said.

"May your eyes see only goodness!" he replied.

After that they spoke the riddling speech. Cuchulainn looked at the swelling of Emer's breasts above her dress.

"A fair land where a warrior might lay his weapon," he said.

"To visit this land a man must have killed a hundred men at every ford from Scenmenn to Banchuing," said Emer.

"In that fair land I'll lay my weapon," said Cuchulainn.

"To visit this land a man must achieve the hero's salmon-leap bearing double his weight in gold. After that he must achieve this feat three times, which is to strike down three times three men leaving the middle man standing."

"In that fair land I'll lay my weapon," said Cuchulainn.

"To visit this land a man must go from Samhain to Imbolc, from Imbolc to Beltain and from Beltain to Lughnasadh without sleep," replied Emer.

"All that you ask is already done," said Cuchulainn.

APPLE—THE TREE OF LOVE
AND PARADISE

The apple tree, or *quert*, was highly magical. The apple has long been a symbol of love, but to the Celts it also symbolised the Otherworld. When the faerie maiden wished to lure Connla to the Land of Youth she threw him an apple. Eating it made him pine for her so much that he followed her willingly to the world of faerie. In another story, King Cormac mac Art was offered a magic silver branch bearing nine apples. When shaken, the apples made a music that lulled all who heard it into a sweet sleep of forgetfulness.

The apple is linked with the element of water. It also protects against evil magic. Apples were used at the festival of Samhain to guard against the powers of evil spirits. This custom survives today in the practice of bobbing for apples on Hallowe'en night. Like the hazel, the apple tree was considered highly sacred by the Celts. Felling it carried the death penalty.

> Mystical Quert, enchanted apple tree,
> beneath your boughs young love lies free.
> Your fragrant fruit in faerie hand
> lured Connla to your timeless land.
>
> Your magic silver branch red-belled
> with nine ripe apples sweetly swelled,
> made faerie music in Manannan's hand
> and sent forgetful slumber over all the land.

How Grainne Won Diarmuid

And after he had the *Ball Seirc*, the love-spot, planted on his brow, Diarmuid used to go about with his cap pulled down over it, for any woman seeing it would fall in love with him. But when the dogs were fighting and he was parting them, his cap lifted so that Grainne saw the Ball Seirc and at once fell deeply in love with him. Then she knew she would leave Finn Mac Cumhail and break her betrothal to him. Calling Diarmuid apart, she asked him to elope with her.

"I will not do that, Lady," he replied, mindful of his loyalty to Finn.

"Then I will put a *geis* on you," said she.

"Lady," said Diarmuid, "I will not go with you. I will neither take you in softness nor in hardness, neither without nor within; I will not take you on horseback or on foot."

And he went away from her.

But she came after him and found him in his house. When he opened the door he saw that she stayed between the two sides of the door and sat astride a billy goat.

"Now Diarmuid," said she, "I am neither without nor within, I am neither on foot nor on horseback. And now you must come with me."

THE MONK'S MISTRESS

The mistress that calls me on a windy night
is the sweet bell at matins.
I would rather be summoned by its delicate peal
than by a wanton woman.

THE FIRST NIGHT

After Cuchulainn had performed the tasks set for him by Emer, he arrived at Emain Macha and Emer was brought to him. All the Ulstermen welcomed her, but Bricriu, the poison-tongued, reminded them that it was the King's right to have the "first forcing" of any new bride in Ulster. He said it would go hard with Cuchulainn to have to let his wife sleep with the King. At this Cuchulainn's anger rose to such a pitch that his cushion burst beneath him, scattering feathers in all directions.

Then Cathbad the Druid said it was a great difficulty because, though King Conchobar could not refuse to sleep with Emer, Cuchulainn would surely kill him for it. To cool him down, Conchobar ordered Cuchulainn to gather all the herds of flocks and swine in that place and bring them to the green at Emain Macha. Meanwhile the men debated the matter and came to this decision, that Emer would sleep that night in the King's bed but that Fergus and Cathbad would also sleep in it. Cuchulainn agreed to this and next day King Conchobar paid him the honour-price for Emer. After that night Cuchulainn and Emer slept together, nor were they parted again before they died.

THE THREE LIGHTEST HEARTS

A student who reads his psalms,
a boy who abandons his childish clothes,
a maiden who has just been made a woman.

SUMMER

BELTAIN was the third Celtic lunar festival. It is named after Bel, the Gaulish god of light, fire and healing, and means "Bel's fire." The festival was celebrated on or around 1 May, and stands midway between the spring equinox and midsummer. It was the time when the Goddess and her consort consummated their union. It marked the beginning of summer, the season of the full flowering of the fertility of the earth when the Maiden aspect of the Goddess became the Mother. It was the season when the work of planting seeds was ended and the time of waiting and encouraging the earth to produce new crops, had arrived.

Agriculturally, it was the time when the herds of sheep and cattle were let out to pasture again. On the day of the festival cattle were driven between two balefires, singeing their hides so that they were purified and cleansed of the risk of

Beltain

disease. In Ireland, holy fires known as *tein-eigin* were made by rubbing together two sticks of sacred wood. The night before Beltain, all fires were extinguished throughout the land, after which the first tein-eigin was kindled by the *Ard Ri*, or High King, on the Hill of Tara, the sacred centre of Ireland. As soon as its flames leapt into the air on hillside after hillside answering bale-fires appeared, until the whole land blazed with these offerings to the fire-god.

Then the fertility rites began. Naked men and women jumped the flames to draw to themselves the powers of procreation. Rituals of the mating of the May Queen with her King consort were enacted. Young couples were allowed to go off into the woods to make love for it was believed that their sexual exuberance would awaken and empower the fertility of the earth. The customs of morris dancing and of dancing round the maypole derive from these fertility rites.

At Beltain, too, men and women would bathe naked in water, rolling in the pre-dawn dew, or dipping their heads and faces in fresh springs and wells. Water was believed to be particularly charged with healing and health-giving properties at this time. Wells and springs were decked with garlands, and cloths and ribbons were hung from nearby trees. On this day, too, flowers were picked and used to braid women's hair or decorate the home, and branches, such as rowan, apple and hazel, were gathered and taken indoors. The hawthorn, or faerie tree, which was normally considered too sacred to cut, was allowed to be culled at Beltain, and its branches brought into the house.

Beltain also marked the beginning of the season of hunting and fighting. For those who had spent the spring months in training, Beltain festivities included contests to try the skills of young would-be warriors, as well as all the dancing, feasting and general merrymaking.

Beltain was the gateway to summer, the counterpart of the festival of Samhain. As at Samhain, therefore, Beltain night was also believed to be a time of communion with the spirit world. This time, instead of ancestral spirits, it was the faerie folk, or sidhe, who were believed to be wandering abroad.

In fact the sidhe held sway over the whole summer season. Celtic myths abound with tales of faerie women, and occasionally faerie men, appearing on the earth at this time, seeking to entice mortals to Tir na n'Og, the Summerlands or the Land of Youth. Finn mac Cumhail's son Oisin, famously followed the faerie Niamh to this land, returning to Ireland to find that three hundred years had passed. Connle also followed a faerie woman to such a land, located beneath the sea, where it is said he found the Well of Wisdom. Although such faerie women were often dangerous, warriors chose to take the risk and journey there because the spiritual gifts of the Otherworld were considered to be beyond price.

For the Celts, the summer season was the jewel of the turning year, and at its height was the midsummer solstice, the longest day of the year when the sun reached its zenith. This great Celtic fire festival took place around 21 June. It is thought to have been celebrated by druids gathered in the great monolithic circle of Stonehenge. They would greet the first rays of the sun by cheering, banging drums and blowing horns. Again, bonfires were lit in honour of the sun-god, and staffs and wands were cut from sacred trees, which the Celts believed were especially imbued with the sun's power on this day. Wooden wheels were set alight and rolled down hillsides and there was much rejoicing and celebration in honour of the sun's great potency. For this was the sun's great moment of victory, the triumph of light over the forces of darkness. This was also the time when the two great trees, the Oak and the Holly, contended for the crown. At midsummer, the Oak triumphed, reigning until midwinter.

The meditations for this season focus on the Mother aspect of the Goddess, fertility, love and marriage, the sun-god, solar energy, smithcraft, and the element of fire. Also with druids and druidesses, journeys to the Otherworld, the *sidhe*, sacred trees of the season, animals and birds with solar affinities, symbolic colours and shapes, warrior feats, battles, hunting, the music of the *sidhe*, and the full flowering of nature.

THE SACRED ELEMENT OF FIRE

Element of fire, radiant one of illumination, inspirer of men. Power of the divine. Potent, solar one, destroyer and regenerator, messenger between the living and the dead. Druids raise you at their festivals, cattle are driven through your flames for purifying. The sacred blacksmith tames your blazing, calling on your power and forging magic weapons for the gods. Bright initiator, inspiring new creation. Insight strikes from you like lightning. Active, phallic one of zeal and passion. Sender of flame and smoke from burning altars, incense of the gods. Spark of divine and Otherworldly wisdom, luminous visionary, sublime sustainer. Inspirer of the secret inner spirit, flame of truth. God of the hearth, transformer of elements, empowering the great cauldron. Light-giver, radiant halo of the gods. Vigorous, volatile one of thrust and anger, forceful vehicle of change. Druids draw on you for fiery knowing and prophetic intuition. South is your direction and the spear of Lugh your symbol.

THE FIERY SPEAR OF LUGH

> Fiery Spear of Lugh, of the many skills,
> Spear that can find its prey unerringly
> Cast by the Lord of Light
> Branch of prophetic gift and fiery utterance.

When the Tuatha de Danann first came to Ireland, the third magic gift they brought with them was the fiery Spear of Lugh. Lugh was the god of light, linked with the sun and solar energy. His feast-day was celebrated at Lughnasadh. The sun was a symbol of the active male principle, and phallic weapons were related to it. Lugh's spear was said to be of such burning power that it had to be set upside down with its head enclosed in the great cauldron to prevent it causing widespread destruction. The union of male and female is explicit in this image, the active and aggressive power of the male being curbed by the passive, all-encompassing watery female principle. It also denotes the vessel of creation receiving the divine spark that energises life. The great Arthurian symbols of the lance and the grail derive from the magical Celtic spear and cauldron. The Celtic wand was closely related to the spear, being the spiritual weapon of the Druids. Wands were also linked with fire and the active masculine principle.

THE MAKING OF BLODEUWEDD

Then Gwydion and Math took it upon themselves to make a wife for Lleu by charms and illusions, out of flowers. They took blossoms of the oak, blossoms of the broom and blooms of the meadowsweet. Then they closeted themselves in a darkened room and raised the wild spells of the woodland, spells of vein and leaf, of petal and branch, of moss and lichen, and they bound into them the close spells of flesh and hand and eye, of breast and beating heart, of brow and lips and hair. Then they called up the breath of life which came first as a wind and then as a little breeze, and filled out her lungs like the sails of a ship. She faltered once and then she took breath, and afterwards, when life was fully in her, she glowed with the richness of the land. They called her Blodeuwedd, which means "Flower-face." When Lleu first set eyes on the woman that was made for him, he was astonished at her beauty. And soon afterwards preparations began for the marriage feast.

May-Time

Time of May, season of loveliness,
full-throated blackbirds welcome the sun's new beams.

The cuckoo sounds a welcome to the summer.
It soothes the memory of the bitter weather
while the bare branches become a thorny hedge.

Summer dries up the little streams, the cattle
seek out water, the heather spreads its long hair,
and the white grass blooms.

The sea is smooth, the ocean is asleep,
the world is covered in flowers.

Bees carry heavy pollen on their feet,
cattle go up the mountain,
the ant finds a rich feast.

The harp of the forest sounds its music
its notes bring peace.
Colours have descended on the hills
and a mist over the lake.

The corncrake squawks, a tireless poet,
the rushing waterfall greets the warm pool with song
and rushes whisper.

Delicate swallows flit through the air,
music is on the hillside,
the fruit is all in bud.

Lovely is the season, full of fresh delight,
winter's chill wind is gone,
the woods are bursting with new life,
joy and tranquillity are come at last.

TREES

The Celtic practice of communing with trees is still remembered by us when we use the expression "to touch wood." When the Celts touched the trees they were connecting with their inner spirits, which later became known as dryads. Stretching from deep within the earth and up to the heavens, trees have long been regarded as bridges between the physical and spiritual worlds. It is this belief that lies behind Ygdrassil, the great Tree of Life of Norse legend. The Celts venerated the ash in a similar way. In Welsh myth, the boy prince Lleu Llaw Gyffes undergoes a death and regeneration experience in such a tree. Echoes of these beliefs are found in Christianity.

On a practical level, trees were indispensable to the Celts. They offered shelter and protection and provided fuel for their fires. They also provided wood for furniture and musical instruments. Mystically, the Celts believed that different trees had particular properties and gifts. They were also regarded as storehouses of memory. Wands and staffs were cut from living trees and, in Druid hands, their powerful energies were used for protection, inspiration and healing.

Hawthorn—the Tree of Fertility

The hawthorn, or *huathe*, is a small tree and belongs to the rose family. In spring it is laden with heavy white blossom which gives a powerful and erotic perfume. It is therefore associated with May celebrations and fertility. Garlands are made from it and used to decorate houses and hang on the maypole at the Beltain celebrations. The hawthorn presides over courtship and marriage. It is linked with the Goddess, who emerges in her Spring Maiden form at this time. Often growing close to springs or wells, it lends a special magic to these places of petitioning and healing. The hawthorn staff planted on Wearyall Hill at Glastonbury by Joseph of Arimathea famously blossoms at Christmas. This sacred tree announces spring, new life, hope, gladness and celebration.

Huathe, little whitethorn tree,
fire-wreathed, white-blossomed guardian of fertility.
Your perfumed offerings breathe new life—
spring-born vitality; your garlands
crown the maypole; underneath your boughs
the young find love and comfort. With your flowers
the new-made Goddess clothes herself.
You weave your faerie spells
by overhanging springs and sacred wells,
and lend your slender wands
to wish-rags, ribbons, festive offerings.
Bringer of nature's pleasures, ushering in
gladness and celebration,
heart's empowering

THE THREE NOBLE STRAINS

The three most famous harpers were the three sons of Uaithne, harper to the Dagda. Their mother was the goddess Boann, a child of the *sidhe*. Her sons took their names from her in this way. When she was in labour with the eldest, her pains were bitter, therefore she called him *Goltraiges*, which means weeping. The second birth was easier and brought her joy so she named the baby *Gentraiges*, meaning laughter; while the third brought weariness so she called him *Suantraiges*. These three sons were named for the Three Noble Strains of music in Ireland, the grief-strain, the joy-strain and the sleep-strain which had power even to death, over men and women, cattle and other creatures at that time.

The Harps of the Sons of Uaithne

When the harpers, the three sons of Uaithne, were invited to play, they uncovered their harps. These had an outer casing of otterskins bound with thongs of Parthian leather set with gold and silver decorations. Their inner coverings were made of pure white kidskin with grey eyes at the centre. The strings themselves were wrapped in linen soft as swansdown. The harps were rare and precious, fashioned out of gold and silver and white bronze and having on them figures of gilded animals—serpents, birds and dogs. When the harpers played, the resonance of the strings caused these gilded animals to circle round them. First the brothers played the Goltraige, the noble Grief-strain. Immediately, all the company began weeping and, when it was ended, twelve men were found to have died of grief.

THE HARP

Harp of Cnoc I Chosgair
you bring soothing and sleep
to the restless —
your curved form
the thrilling of your strings
woken by skilled fingers.
O, excellent red instrument
brimming with melody.

You draw the bird from its flock.
You restore the mind
brown-speckled instrument
of passion and gentleness.

You heal the hurt warrior
and bring joy and beguilement
to women. Mystical one,
you guide the soul
over dark-blue waters.

Harp of the Race of Conn
you are above all instruments
bringing the rest to silence —
pleasing, plaintive, golden-brown.

You are the darling
of sages, sweet-tongued, restless,
blazing crimson star on the faerie hills,
breast-jewel of the High King.

Rich brown harp of poets
your frame is loved by hosts
and the melody that lingers on it.

In your golden mouth is the cry
of faerie women from the faerie mound.
For you are peerless in sound
your sweet-stringed melody —
the highest music.

THE WOMAN ON HORSEBACK

When Pwyll saw the hill of Arberth, they told him: "If anyone of royal blood sits here, he will either receive a blow or see a marvel."

"I will take my chances," replied Pwyll and sat on the hill.

At once a woman on a pale horse, wearing a robe of gold brocade rode slowly towards them. Pwyll sent a man to find out who she was. He followed her on foot but, though she rode slowly, he was unable to catch up with her. Then he fetched his horse and chased after her, but still he was unable to catch her. The next day they returned to the hill and again the woman appeared. This time the man followed her on the fastest horse they had, yet he was still unable to catch up with her. The following day, Pwyll followed her himself, but finding her, again, just out of reach, he called out, "Lady, please stop!" Immediately she reined in her horse, turned towards him, and threw the veil from her head. Pwyll thought he had never in his life seen a more beautiful face. "What is your name?" he asked.

"Rhiannon," she replied.

"And what is your errand?"

"I have come because of my love for you," she said.

The Fenians and the Faerie Hill

Finn and the Fianna were out hunting and six of them chased a beautiful faun to the Mount of Aighe. There the faun disappeared, leaving them to endure a heavy snowfall. Finn asked Cailte if he could find them shelter for the night. Cailte went over the hill and before long found himself looking into a mound of the *sidhe*. It was illuminated and he could see the feasting of the faerie hosts inside, raising pale gold drinking horns and delicate glass cups to their lips. Cailte entered the mound and sat himself on a crystal chair. Around him were twenty-eight warriors, and beside each one a beautiful yellow-haired woman who tended and served him. In the middle of the hall sat a golden-haired woman playing a harp and singing. Whenever she ended a song a horn of sweet wine was handed to her. Then a girl came up to Cailte and offered to wash his feet, but Cailte would not allow it until Finn should come. Then said the company: "Go and bring Finn, for no one has been refused hospitality in his house, therefore he shall not lack it here."

A FAERIE HOUSE

A house I have, it lies in the north
the upper half is red gold
and the lower half is silver.
The entrance hall is made of polished bronze,
its floor is copper.
The roof is thatched with yellow birds' wings,
in the centre of the house is found a pure white candle
with a precious jewel and golden candlesticks.
No sadness or old age is in that place,
the hair stays gold with curling locks,
and there is chess-playing and good companionship,
a ready hospitality for all who come.

PWYLL MEETS ARAWN

One day Pwyll, lord of Dyfed, was out hunting. He became separated from his men and, while listening for his hounds, heard the baying of another pack coming towards him. They were following a stag and brought it down in the clearing where he was waiting. These hounds were like no others he had ever seen, for each dog had luminous white fur and glowing red ears. Even so, Pwyll drove off the pack so that his own hounds might have the deer. Then he saw a rider approaching on a huge dappled grey horse.

"Chieftain, I will not greet you," said the rider.

"Is it your rank that prevents you?" asked Pwyll.

"It is not that, but the discourtesy you have done me in taking for yourself what was the kill of my hounds."

"How can I make amends?" asked Pwyll."

"I am Arawn, Lord of Annwn," replied the other, "and you may make amends if you will, but you must rid me of my enemy Havgan, and furthermore you must exchange places with me for a year and a day. But if you do this you will have the most beautiful woman in the world to grace your bed each night."

Then Pwyll agreed and the men exchanged places.

THE HORNED ONE

The Lord of the Beasts is an ancient and primitive god. In the *Mabinogion*, Owein, one of Arthur's knights, encounters him on a mound, surrounded by ferocious animals. He has one leg and carries a great club. With it he delivers a blow to a stag who bellows in pain. The stag's cry brings to the mound thousands of creatures who gather round their fierce lord and bow to him in homage. Another Celtic image of the Lord of the Beasts is found on the Gundestrup Cauldron. He sits cross-legged, wearing anglers and flanked by a stag, a bull, a hound and a boar. In one hand he holds a torc, in the other a ram-headed snake. He is Cernunnos, the horned god, and the stag is his totem animal. He later became known as Herne the Hunter, the Lord of the Wild Hunt, who was believed to bear the spirits of the dead away to the Otherworld. So widespread was the Celtic worship of the horned god that the early Church felt obliged to discredit him by turning him into the Devil.

Black, club-wielding
Woodman,
one-eyed giant
single-footed.
Wild beasts bow
to your command.

Antlered Ward
of ancient forces.
Green one,
horned one,
fearful god.

THE SACRED STAG OR *DAMH*

The stag is associated with Cernunnos, Lord of the Beasts, who wears antlers and is usually depicted with the stag beside him. Its attributes are dignity, majesty, command and independence. It has an ancient lineage, being one of the oldest creatures in the world, and in Welsh mythology assists in the finding of Mabon, the young son. The Celts partook of the stag's power by wearing its hide as a cloak and sporting its horns on their heads. Considered both regal and divine, the stag was connected with the sun, being sometimes depicted with the rays of the sun as its antlers. The stag's antlers also represented the branches of trees. The potency, aggression and sexual prowess of the stag are tempered by its nobility. The stag holds sway over other wild animals and, as an inner guardian, can be called on to contain and govern the wilder inner emotions.

THE DRUIDIC ORDER

The highest order was that of the druid and required twenty years of training. The Druids were a highly knowledgeable and priestly class. Once trained, they often married and were given secular as well as religious authority. They advised kings and administered the laws of the realm. Mystically they presided over the sacred rituals in groves and stone circles, and were able to call up winds and make other weather changes. Although exempt from war, they assisted supernaturally during battles, such as uttering curses against the enemy and raising up mists. They also made prophetic deductions from natural phenomena such as the shape of clouds or the number and flight of birds, or from patterns in entrails and offerings.

Being philosophers, the Druids taught astronomy, religion and natural science. Caesar tells us that "they held long discussions about the heavenly bodies and their movements, the size of the universe and of the earth, the physical constitution of the world, and the power and properties of the gods." They believed that both the human soul and the universe were indestructible, and that the soul passed into the Otherworld after death. Their central philosophy was: "To honour the gods, to do no evil and to practise courage."

THE GIFTS OF THE FAERIE PEOPLE

After the time when the giant races, the Firbolgs and the Fomorians, ruled over Ireland, a new race came. They came from the west travelling over the water like a mist. They called themselves the *Tuatha de Danann* after their great mother, the Goddess Danu. The Dagda was their chief god and later his sovereignty passed to his son Lugh. On arrival the Tuatha brought four magic gifts with them. The *lia fail* from the city of Falias, the Sword of Nuada from the city of Gorias, the Spear of Lugh from the city of Finias, and the Cauldron of the Dagda from the city of Murias. The Tuatha overcame the Fomorians in the two great battles of Mag Tuiread. They were later overcome in their turn by the Milesians under their leader Amergin, the poet seer. The Tuatha surrendered the land to them but were allowed to remain underground, where they lived on in the hills and burial mounds. After this they became known as the *sidhe*, or faerie people.

THE GENEROSITY OF THE SIDHE

A boy appeared before the three sons of the king,
a young lad of wonderful appearance,
his beard was forked and brown, long curls
of golden hair cascaded down his shoulders,
fastened by fine gold threads to stop it
blowing in the wind; his sandal
was purest silver, nor did the foot within it
scatter the dew-drops on the grass-blades
as he walked on them.
He came to the men and greeted them.
"Where are you from?" they asked him,
"The dew-covered, gleaming *Bruig*," he said.
"What is your name?" they asked,
"Bodb Derg, son of the Dagda. Come with me!"
He led them to the *Bruig* and seated them
in chairs of crystal. When food was offered
they refused, asking instead a king's inheritance.
At this those in the mound fell silent, while in their hands
were golden and silver horns and cups and goblets.
Then the *sidhe* took counsel and decided they would help them.
So they gave them wives and wealth, weapons and land.

And Aengus the Og gave them a royal estate
while Bodb Derg offered them his best musician.
After that the King's sons stayed in the mound
a full three days and nights before they went their way
laden with wealth and blessings from the sidhe.

How the Brown Bull of Cuailnge was Lost through Careless Talk

After Queen Medbh heard that the Brown Bull of Cuailnge was the equal of Finnbennach, her husband's bull, she sent to ask Dáire of Ulster if she might borrow the Brown Bull for a year. "Tell him," she said, "that at the end of the year I will give him the bull back again, also fifty heifers and a portion of land, a chariot of great worth and, if that is not enough, tell him he may enjoy the friendliness of my own thighs."

When these terms were put to Dáire he jumped on his cushion until the seams burst. "On my soul," he exclaimed, "whatever the Ulstermen say, I'll have this treasure!" Then the messengers were offered the best hospitality. They feasted and drank until their tongues were loosened. Later that night they were overheard saying: "It is just as well that Dáire has consented to the terms, for otherwise it would have taken the might of four provinces of Ireland to carry the bull out of Ulster." When this was reported to Dáire he became very angry and refused to release the bull. But after it was told to Medbh she vowed to take the bull by force. Thus began the terrible story of the *Tain Bo Cuailnge*, the Cattle Raid of Cooley.

The Solar Wisdom of the Eagle

The power of the sun, intellect, the air, masculine strength, wisdom and courage, all reside in the eagle or *iolair*. Shamans wore cloaks and head-dresses made of eagle feathers. Annually at Beltain sixty druids were believed to gather on an island in Loch Lomond in the form of eagles in order to interpret the augurs for the following year. The eagle was said to guard the summit of the World Tree, while the snake guarded its root. In Welsh myth, Lleu shapechanges into an eagle at death and perches on the top of an oak until Gwydion sings him down through the power of the *englyn*, or magical verse.

Mighty sun king,
hanging high
above snowy mountain peaks
while far below, the bellied earth
beast-burdened, falls away.
Bright-winged one,
potent is your flight,
your eyes perceive the truth.
You breast the sky
and crown the Cosmic Tree,
spanning the heavens and
swooping to earth's chthonic
energies. In your feathered cloaks
shamanic druids rise
and enter airy realms
of truth and sovereignty.

THE MIDSUMMER SOLSTICE

21 June

*A*ll night the ancient ring of stones and dolmens hums its energies. Dawn's faint light lifts the darkness, a rosy halo rises above the skyline, and now the sun's first beam strikes through the granite archway. Hail sun-god, bearer of light and power. Hail, bright deity, ascending the zodiacal arch, and reaching the zenith of the year. Druids welcome you with drumming, blowing of curling horns. The crowning of the year is yours, the time of greatest force and potency. Birch, fennel, white lilies and trefoil are your early offerings. Bonfires are lit, holy men cut staffs and wands from hazel, birch and willow. The trees of summer, charged by your fullness, hold your most potent magic. Day of feast and celebration, honouring of the oak, the Summer King, with rolling of fiery wheels. Now is the dark diminished. Mabon, the sacred child, is victor. Divine Light, shining god in brightest splendour, reaches to fullest glory.

Finn and the Mound of the Sidhe

When Finn and the Fianna were at Badamair, camping near the Suir, one of the sidhe used to come out at night from the faerie mound on Femen and steal their meat from the cooking-pot. This happened twice but on the third night Finn was waiting for him beside the mound, and as the man was carrying the food into the knoll, Finn caught hold of him so that he fell. Then a faerie woman came out, holding a vessel of drink in her hand and, seeing Finn, she went quickly to close the door of the knoll, but Finn stuck his thumb between the door and the wooden post. After that he took it out and put it in his mouth. At once he began to sing an incantation. When he had finished his *imbas* he returned to the Fianna. But ever after that time, if he put his thumb in his mouth he was able to see beyond the range of human seeing and to know beyond the range of human knowing.

ETAIN

A woman by a spring
wetting her hair in a silver bowl
the bowl adorned with four gold birds, and rimmed
with purple jewels of carbuncle.
A fleecy purple cloak upon her
and a brooch of silver filigree to hold it.
A hooded green silk dress with intricate design
and twisting animals on brooch and ornament.
The sunlight striking on the gold-work
and the shining silk. Her yellow hair
parted in two halves and braided on her head
glowing like polished gold.
As she unbraids it, her arms and shoulders
lift through her slitted dress
shimmering white and soft as untouched snow,
her skin is clear as dew, her cheeks deep-hued
as foxgloves. Like the beetle's wing her eyebrow,
like a shower of pearls in brightness her white teeth.
Blue as the bugloss are her eyes,
her lips vermilion, long and white her fingers,
her arms, her side, white as the foamy wave.

Her thighs so sleek and glossy, and her knees
supple and firm, her shins and heels straight and true.
The moon is in her face, nobility in her brow,
the dart of love plays in her eye, so fair is she,
so radiant, that they thought she was a faerie.

THE MOTHER OF OISIN

Finn awoke and saw a woman of great beauty standing over him. "I am Saab," she said, "I was the fawn you chased today. The Dark Druid of the *sidhe* turned me into that shape because I refused to love him. But I was told that if I could reach Finn's house in the Dun of Allen, my human form would be restored. Then Saab stayed with Finn and became his wife and such was the love between them that Finn neglected the hunt and the battles of the Fianna, wishing only to be by her side. But one day he was summoned to defend the shores of Erin. When he returned, he found that Saab had gone. Finn searched for her in vain for seven long years until one day as he was hunting on Ben Bulben, in Sligo, his hounds cornered a naked boy with long, wild hair. The boy was dumb and frightened but Finn took him home and after a time he regained his speech. He told Finn he had lived with his mother, a fawn, who left him to follow a dark man who struck her with a hazel wand. Ever after, Finn's son was known as Oisin, meaning "Little Fawn."

SACRED NUMBERS—FIVE

The number five is composed of the number four—which denotes matter and material existence, with the number one, which is a unifying and spiritual number. Five is therefore a mystical number. The five streams outflowing from the Well of Wisdom corresponded to the five senses, through which the sacred knowledge and wisdom of the hazelnuts and the salmon may be absorbed. There were also five provinces of Ireland, Meath being the fifth and central one which united the four others. Thus Meath was the County of Sacred Sovereignty and the spiritual heart of Ireland. It was there that the Seat of the High King was founded on the Hill of Tara. Today, in Celtic-style meditation or ritual, it is common to set up a small table with objects in each of its corners to symbolise the four directions and the elements that correspond to them. These could be a stone to symbolise the north, a seed-ball for the east, an incense stick for the south and a cup of water for the west. The centre is therefore left bare for a fifth and more spiritual object, such as a candle, which draws the others into a mystical pattern of wholeness.

THE OTHERWORLD

One day Connle the Redhaired was out riding with his father when a woman approached them dressed in a strange garment. Connle asked her where she had come from and she told him her home was in *Tir na n'Og*, The Land of Youth. Then she said: "Come with me, Connle the Redhaired, with your bejewelled neck and eyes like candle flame!" She told him the delights of the land and then threw him an apple and vanished. For a month afterwards he ate nothing but the apple and sickened for the woman. She came to him again, and this time he followed her. She led him to a jewelled boat and he climbed in and sailed away with her. After that he was never seen on this earth again.

Conle listened like a man entranced
while the silk-voiced maiden
told him of Tir na n'Og, the Land of Youth.
"Come with me," she said, "and let me take you
where the rainbow-feathered birds of Rhiannon
fill the sweet air with rich enchanted melody,
where welling streams of purplish-blue
wind through the fringes of the grassy woods,
where brown-tilled plains display their yellow curling crops,
where water-meadows lie, and deep, cool-breasted lakes
mirror the cloud-waved sky, where gentle winds
flutter the golden plumage of the dew-bright leaves.
In such a land no sickness enters,
all is love and laughter, song and feasting.
There lies the sacred Well of Wisdom
crowned with the hazel-trees of Inspiration."
Then she breathed on him, the hapless son of Conn.
Her breath was apple-sweet and fragrant.
Connle sighed once, looked one last time on earth,
then turned his horse and followed where she led.

THE ORACULAR HEAD OF BRAN

After the great battle between Wales and Ireland, only seven warriors escaped alive. Chief of them was Bran, the great King of Wales, but he was wounded in the foot with a poisoned dart and knew that he would die. Then Bran ordered his men to cut off his head and carry it with them to London. He said that on the way his head would speak to them and advise them as before. He told them that they must spend seven years at Harlech and a further eighty years in Pembroke while his head addressed them. They did this and in that time, a time suspended in the Otherworld, they enjoyed such feasting, and such entertainment from conversing with Bran's head, that they forgot all sorrow. Afterwards they journeyed on to London and buried the head on White Hill, facing out to France, where Bran undertook to protect the nation. Bran's totem animal being the raven, it is said to this day that if ever the ravens desert the Tower of London, Britain will fall.

ROWAN—THE TREE OF LIFE

The rowan, or *luis*, is related to the rose family, along with the apple tree, which is also linked to the Otherworld. The rowan likes high altitudes and, because its leaves resemble those of the ash, it is also called the mountain ash. A delicate and feminine tree, it is quite small and in spring its branches are bowed down with clusters of white flowers. Later its bright red berries provide a feast for birds. In winter its bare moonlit form was also revered. A mystical tree, its branches were used by druids for incense and divination. Spindles and spinning wheels were made from it and sprigs of it were worn to protect against abduction to the faerie Land of Youth.

Delicate Luis, lively rowan tree,
your honeyed berries breaking on the tongue
bring youthfulness and life. Light, mystic one
your boughs sweet-smoke with incense.
In their haze bright, summoned spirits
pass between the worlds.
Fair, goddess-flowered, oracular
your groves speak female wisdom while your rods
spin threads of life. Your subtle, scented fruits
drew Grainne in her quickening. Sacred moon-tree,
druid-favoured, when your limbs are bare
on frosted nights your head
holds starlight.

THE BIRDS OF RHIANNON

It was said that the beautiful singing of the Birds of Rhiannon could be heard at the threshold of the Otherworld. When Bran's men began their years of feasting and entertainment with his oracular head, they heard the singing of these birds, which was the sign that they had entered the Otherworld. Rhiannon was a faerie woman and the wife of Pwyll, Lord of Annwn. It was said that her birds could bring the dead back to life, and the living into a sleep like death. This account is echoed in Irish myth, for Cliodna, wife of the sea-god Manannan, also had three mystical birds. One was blue with a crimson head, one was red with a green head, and the third was speckled with a gold head. The gifts of Cliodna's three birds were instruction, entertainment and healing sleep. But rare it was to hear the singing of any such birds for, as the Welsh triad tells us:

There are three things which are not often heard:

> the song of the birds of Rhiannon,
> wisdom from the mouth of a Saxon,
> the invitation of a miser to a feast.

THE THREE POISONED STONE SPEARS

When Ysbaddaden's eyelids were propped up with forks, he was able to see Culhwch, and his retinue with him. Ysbaddaden snatched up one of his three stone spears and threw it at them. But Bedwyr caught it and hurled it back, striking the giant in the knee. "What is that, a gadfly sting!" shouted the giant "Curses on you, for now I shall feel stiffness whenever I walk uphill!" A second time the men came before the giant and a second time he threw a spear at them. But Menw caught it and hurled it back, so that it went straight through Ysbaddaden's chest. "Curse you for that leech-bite!" stormed the giant, "Now when I walk uphill I shall be plagued by chest pains, stomach pains and loss of appetite!" A third time they approached him, and begged him not to shoot at them. But as they were departing, he threw a third spear at them. Culhwch caught it and hurled it at the giant's eyeball. "Curses on you, my would-be son-in-law!" shouted Ysbaddaden. "Now whenever the wind blows on my face, my eyes will water. And I will suffer headaches and dizziness every new moon, because of you!"

SACRED SYMBOLS—THE TRIANGLE

To the Celts the power of three was a very mystical concept. They regarded the shape of a triangle, especially an equilateral triangle, as holding three aspects in harmony. While two points denoted simple duality, the third allowed a mystical element to enter the equation. Thus the equilateral triangle symbolised proportion, the harmony of three and the realm of divinity. In ancient understanding, the properties of the equilateral triangle were also related to the elements. An upward pointing triangle represented fire, the active masculine principle and the spiritual ascent to heaven, while one pointing downwards symbolised water, the passive feminine element and the descent of blessing from heaven. The two triangles therefore reflected each other. Put together they formed the six-pointed star, symbol of wholeness and the union of opposites. In early Celtic belief the power of three was linked with the triple-aspected goddess. In Celtic Christianity this concept was transmuted into the Three Marys and, later, into the Christian trinity.

DIVINE POWER OF THE SUN

Great orb, sky-jewel, life-giver, lighter of the land. Splendid, shining one, climbing the heavens, stealing blackness, covering the stars. At the year's waning, entering the cave of death, striking the chamber of darkness, rising to power again. Gold-shedder, bringer of hope, bestower of health, and wielder of strength at the waxing of the year. High knowledge of you is wisdom, the *imbus gréine*, the learning of druids. To them you are the Great Sul, eye of day, unwearying sovereign, *grianainech*, face of Lugh. Light-bringer, lion-maned power of brightness, yellow are your locks, a flowing gold shaken across the earth. Transformer of darkness, waker of the Sleeping Mother, Highest Illuminator.

> Hail to you, Sun of the seasons,
> banisher of darkness.
> Hail to you, strider of the sky,
> illuminator of the souls of men.
> Hail, fire-dancer and earth-waker—
> god of the thousand rays,
> gilding the green-faced land
> and shimmering on the timeless waters
> of the Mother's wisdom.

KING RUADH BREAKS FAITH WITH THE OTHERWORLDLY WOMEN

Ruadh, King of Alba, set out with a fleet of three ships to meet his Norwegian friends. On their way the ships became becalmed, and they found themselves immobile in the middle of the ocean. Votive offerings of gold and costly objects cast into the water proved useless against the magic, so lots were cast for diving into the water, and the lot fell to Ruadh. As soon as the waves closed over him, he found himself on a great plain which stretched away on either side and on it were nine women, each as lovely as the next. "It was we," they said, "who bound your ships so that you would come to us. And to release the magic, we ask that you remain here for nine nights, and take one of us to your bed each night."

Ruadh agreed to this and after nine nights had passed one of the women told him she had conceived a child. She asked him to come back and fetch the son that she would bear him. Then Ruadh and his fleet continued on their journey, staying with their companions for seven years. After that they returned by another route. But just as their ship was coming to land, the women overtook them in a ship of copper. Weeping, they threw a young boy onto the shore, who hit his head on a sharp rock and died. Then the women turned their boat and sailed away.

FINN'S FAERIE HARPER AND
THE MUSIC OF THE SIDHE

When Finn was out hunting in Slievenamon he rested on a grassy mound. Looking round, he saw near him a little man with long yellow hair cascading below his waist, playing a harp that was almost as big as himself. The sound of it was melodious and beguiling. The man stopped playing and came to Finn, offering him his hand, and saying he was of the sidhe. Then he sat between Finn's thighs and played his harp until the Fianna arrived. They were all astonished by the sweetness of the music and praised Finn for discovering such a player. The harper's name was Cnú Deróil, meaning "The Little," Finn called him "Nutlet" and gave him wealth and riches, and Cnú became famous all over Ireland.

Then Finn sent to find a wife for Cnú, and a woman small enough was found for him among the *sidhe*. Her name was Bláthnait and she had the gift of second sight and would reveal to the Fianna what lay in store for them. The couple became a great treasure of the court, and often travelled with the warriors. If they were caught in a storm, Finn would shelter Bláthnait and Cnú under his cloak.

INVITATION FROM THE LORD OF THE FAERIES

Woman of beauty, come to my fair land
where music fills the air, the hair is golden
and the skin like snow. Nothing is hoarded,
teeth shine with whiteness, brows are black,
the hosts are delightful to look upon,
each cheek is crimson as the foxglove.

The colour on the moor is purple,
so fair is the Great Plain
that after seeing it the plains of Ireland
seem like a desert. The ale in that land
is richer than the ale of mortals, nor is old age
known or death encountered.
That kingdom flows with little streams,
in it are found rich-flavoured wine and mead,
the people there are perfect and unblemished.

Though we can see all men,
no mortal man can see us; we are hidden from them.
Fair lady, if you come with me
you will receive a crown of gold,
mead, honey, milk and ale will ever after be your food.

DAHUT AND THE ISLAND OF THE DRUIDESSES

Late that night Dahut, the mermaid's daughter, stole down to the shore and, untying a small coracle, set out across the velvet waters. No sooner was she out into the Bay of the Dead, than the waves became turbulent, tossing her coracle to right and left. But Dahut struck chords on her little harp, and calmed them. By this magic she passed safely to the *Ile de Seine* and left her boat on the shore. Making her way through the dark woods, she came upon a clearing and saw nine druidesses gathered round a fire. Falling to her knees, she begged their help against the Unruly Mother who would drown her city, and the Ferocious Father who would build his church there. The druidesses listened to her requests and afterwards promised to send their elves, the Korrigans, to accomplish two tasks, the building of a dyke to protect the city from flooding, and the building of a castle that would overtop the church. Then they sent Dahut home in safety.

Aspects of the Goddess— the Mother

After renewing herself as the Maiden and choosing her consort, the Goddess of the Land moves into her next aspect, that of the Mother. As the Mother, she is the giver of new life, instigator of the sacred cycle of birth and death, and provider of sustenance. The Mother in Celtic belief often took the title of the Modron and was linked with the sacred son, the Mabon. From the Modron springs the new hero, the bringer of light and consciousness, the sacrificial son. The Mother is also associated with harvest and bounty, often being depicted with a cornucopia filled with fruit, wine and ears of corn. In Welsh mythology Ceridwen, with her Cauldron of Regeneration, is a type of the Mother, giving birth to the poet-seer Taliesin. In Irish myth, Deirdre provides an image of the Sorrowing Mother when Naoise is killed. Although Deirdre is grieving for her husband, in Celtic understanding consort and son were symbolically linked, the one becoming the other in line with the seasonal round.

DEIRDRE REMEMBERING A SCOTTISH GLEN

Glen of gleaming fish-filled pools and fruit-trees,
glen of pointed wheat-waved hills,
I am in sorrow to remember you –
bee-laden and the haunt of wild oxen.

Glen ringing with song of blackbird, thrush and cuckoo,
offering shelter for the fox,
wooded glen of wild scented garlic, watercress,
clover and bright flowers, leafy and curly-headed.

Glen filled with the cries of dappled deer
lying in oak-leaved woodland.

Glen of the rowan's crimson berries
food for each flock of birds
and haven for badgers.

Glen of keen-eyed hawks,
of tall peaks and autumn fruits and berries.
Glen of shiny sleek-formed otters,

of kingly white-winged swans
and spawning salmon.

Glen of curly-branching yews,
dew-sprinkled grass, rich pasturing for cattle.
White-starred, flowery glen in sunlight
dwelling of pearl-white, graceful high-born women.

Symbolic Colours—Red

Red symbolises boldness, blood and passion. For the Celts this meant above all passion in war, and blood spilt in battle-frenzy. Thus the gaelic words for red, *derg* and *ruadh*, were used to describe kings, warriors or gods who were distinguished in battle. Examples include King Ruadh of Alba; Red Hugh, the father of Macha; Fergus mac Roich, leader of the Red Branch Warriors; and the Dagda, also called *Ruadh Rofhessa*, the Great Red Sage, because he cut a swathe through the Fomorians in the Battle of Mag Tuiread.

The colour red is also connected with death in battle. The ill-fated Irish king Conary Mor is under *geis* that: "No three Reds shall go before thee to the house of Red." But when he approaches the hostel of Da Derga, Lord of Leinster, three red-clad men on red horses precede him. These strange riders have come from the faerie mounds and tell him: "Though we are living we are dead." In the bloody battle that ensues, Conary and most of his men are killed.

Red is also linked with fire and with sexuality. Along with black and white, it is one of the Three Mystical Colours that provoke both Deirdre and Peredur into contemplation of their loved ones.

THE MORRIGAN

The Morrigan was the triple-aspected Goddess of Death and Battle. Her three fate-goddesses were Ana, or Black Annis, who was said to drop from a tree like a spider onto her victims, Badbh the Crow who was also the Washer at the Ford, and was seen washing Cuchulain's blood-stained shirt at his last battle, and Macha, the Red or the Raven, who sported the heads of slaughtered men on poles. This triple deity was summoned into battle by the sound of warhorns emulating the cry of ravens, for the raven was an emblem of death. The Morrigan could shapeshift into a raven and in this guise perched on Cuchulainn's shoulder as he died. Before that she had invited Cuchulainn to love her and, when he refused, had set herself against him. Instead of defying the Morrigan, the Celts called on her, accepting her power of death as a necessary aspect of the Goddess.

CELTIC WOMEN IN BATTLE

The Celts were a fierce race, warlike and delighting in battle. They entered battle naked with only their gold torcs about their necks and their shields and weapons in their hands, believing that nakedness conferred a special magic and protection. Added to this, they were accompanied into battle by their druids who rolled their eyes and raised their staffs to heaven and called down magical curses upon the enemy. To the orderly ranks of the Roman soldiers, the conduct of the Celts was fearsome. But the Celtic soldier became even more fearsome if his wife joined him in battle. The Roman writer, Marcellinus, describes the warrior's wife as "stronger than he by far and with flashing eyes." He adds that the Romans especially fear her when she "swells her neck and gnashes her teeth and, poising her huge white arms, proceeds to rain punches mingled with kicks, like shots discharged by the twisted cords of a catapult."

"SUMMER" FROM AMERGIN'S POEM OF THE SEASONS

Summer is the season for long journeys,
silent is the wood of the tall trees
undisturbed by wind,
green is its clothing, a sheltering canopy.
The water sucks and swirls in the stream
and there is warmth now in the very clods of earth.

Symbolic Colours—Green

Green is the colour most commonly associated with the Celts. This is because it is the colour of nature, with which they were intimately connected. Beautiful women such as Etain are described as wearing green dresses. This denotes the maiden aspect of the Goddess, whose fertility causes the land to become clothed in green vegetation. Faerie women were also clad in green which is the colour of the *sidhe*. The power inherent in the colour green is considered by Celtic mystics to emanate from the Green Ray, which symbolises the Western Mystery Tradition. The Green Bough denotes immortality and the Green Man is the symbol of fertility, growth and new life. Green was also the colour of the Otherworld, the Land of Youth, which lay either across the sea or just beneath the waves. Erin is also associated with green, being at one time identified with the Otherworld.

ETAIN BECOMES A BUTTERFLY

After Midhir returned with Etain, his new wife and the most beautiful woman of the land, his first wife, Fuamnach, became very jealous of her. Trained in the Druidic arts, she struck her with a quickentree rod and turned her into a pool of water. But within the water the essence of Etain formed into a pupae from which she emerged as a purple butterfly, the span of her wings being the size of a man's head:

> Fairer than harps and pipes and flutes
> was the sound of her whirring wings,
> her sweet melodious singing.
> Two precious jewels
> the shining of her eyes at night.
> The perfume wafting from her
> banished all thirst and hunger.
> Moisture sprayed from her wings
> healed plague and sickness.
> Fluttering near Midhir's head
> she brought delight and nourishment,
> a radiant joy. And while she stayed by him
> he took no other wife. Then one day
> Fuamnach returned and saw Etain,
> and with her arts raised up a storm

which blew about the beautiful winged creature
for seven long years, until at last
she fell on the breast of Aengus Og
in his house on the Brugh of the Boyne.

THE WILD BOAR OF THE WARRIOR

Boars and pigs were sacred to the Goddess. The wild boar, or *torc*, denoted unbridled strength, ferocity, untamed power and raw energy. Depicted on shields and helmets, it gave the warrior courage, force and daring. Horns fashioned like the gaping mouths of boars and equipped with vibrating wooden tongues, were carried into battle screeching their warnings as the men charged into the enemy. The warrior and the boar were closely bound up with each other. Hunting the wild boar was the test of the best warriors in the land, joints of pork were given as the Hero's Portion at feasts, and choice pieces were buried with chieftains to give them strength in the next world.

Both the boar and the pig were magically linked to the Underworld. In Welsh mythology Gwydion tricks Pwyll into giving up the pigs of Arawn, the gift of the Underworld king, and Culhwch and Arthur pursue the boar Twrch Trwyth in a deadly hunt in which many men are lost before the boar is finally overcome. In Irish myth Diarmuid is killed by the fierce Boar of Ben Bulben, his shapechanged lifelong enemy.

THE QUICKEN TREE

The magical Quicken Tree was an Otherworldly type of rowan tree and, like the rowan, it was believed to have faerie powers of rejuvenation and new life. In the Irish story of Diarmuid and Grainne, the fleeing lovers take refuge in the magic Forest of Dooros, in the heart of which grew a famous Quicken Tree. This was an Otherworldly tree which had grown from a berry dropped by one of the faerie race, the Tuatha de Danann. It was said that the berries tasted of honey and that they conferred joy and youthfulness on those who ate them. The tree was guarded by a giant called Sharvan the Surly who allowed Diarmuid and Grainne to remain in the forest provided they promised not to take a single berry from the tree. All went well until Grainne became pregnant. As the child quickened in her womb, she began to long for the taste of the Quicken berries. The only way Diarmuid could procure them for her was by killing the giant.

O Quicken Tree,
bright-berried one of life and loveliness,
Otherworldly tree of faerie powers,
youth is in your fruit, no woman can resist
your honeyed berries.
Gift-giving one, your power calls out
with thrust of life and young desire of love.
Immortal tree, wellspring of liveliness,
beside your roots, in hindering chains,
the surly life-denying giant crouches.
One-eyed guardian, ogre of malice,
boldness must strike you down,
only in death is found
new life's releasing.

Cormac in the Otherworld

As Cormac set out to find his family, a great mist arose around him. After it cleared he found himself on a wide plain with a fortress in the middle of it. He went inside the fortress and saw three wonders. First he saw horsemen thatching a house with white feathers which blew away with every gust of wind, while yet the horsemen continued thatching. Next he saw a man feeding a fire with branches that burned so fiercely he was never able to rest from his work. After that he came upon a well fringed with hazel trees. All the people of the land were drinking water from it and Cormac joined them. Then Manannan mac Lir, the god of the sea, appeared to him and said that it was he who came with the silver branch. Cormac asked him to explain the wonders. "The horsemen," said Manannan, "are the type of men who spend their time collecting vanities, while the woodman spends too long working for others, never stopping to warm himself. The well is the Well of Inspiration, and it was so that you would drink its waters that I lured you to this land."

THE THREE SOUNDS OF INCREASE

The mooing of a cow with full udder,
the hammering of the smithy,
the strong swish of the plow.

AUTUMN

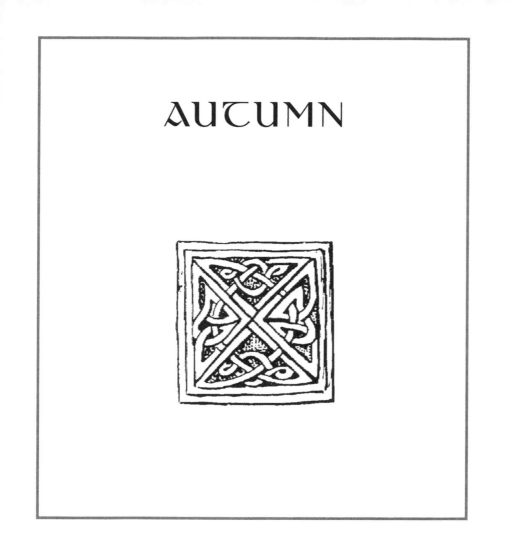

THE fourth great Celtic lunar festival was held around 1 August and named after Lugh, the god of light. It marks the beginning of autumn and was later called *Lammas*, meaning "First Loaf." This is the time when the fruit is ripe and the crops and grain fully grown, the time when the Great Mother delivers her bounty. The festival seems to have been very important. It began a fortnight before the day of the feast and continued for a further fortnight. The Celts had a saying that as long as this festival was observed, there would continue to be corn and milk for every household.

The god Lugh was worshipped all over the Celtic world. He was also called *Lugh Lámfada*, meaning "light of the long arm." Another name for him was the *Ildana*, the many-skilled. A story tells how, as a young god lately come to Ireland, he sought admittance to the court of King Nuada at Tara. He arrived

Lughrasadh

at the palace gate dressed in the robes of a king and demanded entrance. The porter asked for his name and business.

"My name is Lugh," he replied, "and I am a carpenter." The porter told him the court had no need of a carpenter, because they already possessed one. "I am also a harper," said Lugh. Again, the porter said they had a harper. "I am an excellent smith besides," persisted Lugh and proceeded to list all his accomplishments including that of *fili*, warrior, magician, astrologer, cook, physician and storyteller. When the porter replied that all such skills were already represented in the court, Lugh asked him if any there possessed all of them at once. As there was no one to rival him, he was allowed into the court and, once admitted, made such an impression on the Tuatha de Danann, that Nuada yielded him the seat of kingship.

Nasadh means assembly or games, so the festival of Lughnasadh was characterised by games and horse-racing contests and feats of physical prowess as well as the usual feasting and celebration. It marked the high point of a season in which war-skills and hunting were still the order of the day. At the festival, the goddess Tailtiu was honoured. She was the foster-mother of Lugh, and is said to have died from exhaustion after labouring to clear the land near Tara for crop cultivation. Lugh commanded that the people attend a yearly assembly at the sacred plain of Tailltin in her honour. Tailtiu was a type of harvest mother and her self-sacrifice for the good of the land also indicated her Sovereign nature.

At Lughnasadh the first fruits of the harvest were cut down and offered to the gods. Celebration circular dances were performed in which the chiefs of the tribes wore horned headpieces in honour of hunting and physical prowess, and corncakes were baked in the shape of the corn king, Bel, who was treated as a sacrificial god and eaten. The autumn festival was one of plenty and prosperity, of celebration of the fruits of the earth and its bounty. It was also a time when alliances were arranged and marriages contracted. There was also a Celtic system in which a trial marriage could be entered into at Lughnasadh, and if the union proved unhappy, the contract could be dissolved at Beltain.

The god Lugh owned many magical objects and weapons, chief of which was his fiery spear from which his title, the Long Hand, was derived. Lugh was the son of the Dagda, the Good God. Being the son and the god of light, he was regarded as a type of the Mabon, or young son, connected to the Modron, or Mother.

Mother and son feature together in the solar festival, the autumn equinox, that lies at the midpoint of this season, around 21 September. It is the second time in the year when day and night are perfectly balanced. Whereas Lughnasadh heralded the beginning of the harvest, by the time of the autumn equinox the harvest was over. At this festival, grain and other foods and provisions were set aside for storage, and thanksgiving was given for the completion of the year's natural cycle. Again, bonfires were lit, and the cornucopia of the goddess was honoured through feasting, drinking, and general celebration.

Although Tailtiu featured at the celebration of Lughnasadh, as the autumn season progressed, another and much greater goddess began to come into her own. This was Ceridwen, witch-goddess and owner of the magic cauldron. Ceridwen was the unwitting mother of the great Welsh bard, Taliesin, who received his inspired knowledge from the brew conjured in her cauldron. She was associated with grain and with the Greek goddess, Ceres, and also with water and the Otherworld, because of her cauldron.

The cauldron was an important Celtic symbol. It was another of the four sacred gifts, and was brought to Ireland by the Dagda. It had several magic properties. One was abundance, for the Dagda's cauldron never ran out of food, and another was renewal, for in the hands of Bran, King of Wales, it had the power to restore warriors to life. There is also an ancient poem called the *Preiddeu Annwn* in which Arthur and his men set out in their ship Pridwen to bring back a cauldron from the Otherworld. Their aim is to take it from the nine priestesses who guard it and warm its pearly rim with their breath. Only seven men return from the raid, and we are not told if they brought the cauldron with them. In the hands of the goddess Ceridwen, however, the cauldron reveals its greatest powers, for the potion she brews in it contains the three priceless gifts of wisdom, knowledge and intuition.

The cauldron was the symbol of the element of water, which the Celts regarded as the most important of the four elements. All wells, springs, lakes and rivers were considered to be gateways to the Otherworld. Faerie women were connected with water and the Otherworld. Water was therefore a feminine element, source of inspiration, purification and magical understanding. It contained the mystical properties of life itself

The main themes of meditation for this section include the fruitfulness of the land, the sovereignty of the Goddess, Taliesin, the properties of the cauldron, the birth of Deirdre, Dahut, mermaids, sea creatures, trees and animals connected with the season, the element of water, and the contention between Druidism and Celtic Christianity.

INVOCATION TO LUGH

Lugh *Ildana*
god of many skills
bard and healer
music-maker and fire-blazer
adept in the craft of smiths
and in the sacred art of poetry.

Lugh of the radiant face
helper of heroes
invincible in battle
with strength like the sun
full-blazing at noon.

Lugh *Lamfada*
Lugh of the long arm
whose living fiery spear aimed straight
finds out the enemy.
Peerless you sit
in the court of the gods.

THE SACRED ELEMENT OF WATER

Sacred element of water, wellspring of life and mystical gateway to the Otherworld. The damsels of the wells have guarded you, offering you to weary travellers in their golden goblets. Swelling symbol of emotion, origin of life and new creation. Female element, governed by the moon, vast are your oceans, your waves and white-fringed foamings. Formless power of the soul, beneath your filmy depths are found the Summer Lands, realm of the ninefold Goddess. Heart-spring of wisdom, stream of blessing, Connle's well draws inspiration from you. Healing is in your waters, reviving the desert wasteland. Cleanser and renewer, Fountain of Immortality, holy one of spiritual renewal. The Salmon of Knowledge live in your springs. In your depths are dreams and visions yet unborn. Druids have bound and loosed you, seeking inspiration beside your flowing waves. Womb of ancient creatures, West is your direction and the cauldron your sacred symbol.

THE CAULDRON OF THE DAGDA

Cauldron of the Dagda, the Good god,
Vessel of endless nourishment
Transformer of death to life
wherein is rest and newborn mysteries.

The fourth gift brought to Ireland by the Tuatha de Danann was the Cauldron of the Dagda. This magic cauldron, initially belonging to the Dagda, or "Good God," was a vessel of vast size that provided an inexhaustible supply of food. It was the Celtic horn of plenty, a vessel of material and spiritual nourishment. It also possessed the power of regeneration. In the *Mabinogion*, Bran gives the King of Ireland a cauldron which restores dead warriors to life after they are laid in it. The cauldron was also a vessel of magical and inspirational brews. Ceridwen used her witch's cauldron to prepare the three drops of knowledge, wisdom, and intuition, which turned the young boy Gwion into the great bard Taliesin. Connected with the element of water, the most revered of the four elements, the cauldron became a particularly potent symbol of Celtic spirituality. It is also believed to be the prototype of the Holy Grail of Arthurian legend.

THE GOOD GOD

The Dagda was the most gigantic and powerful of the old Irish gods. He was called the Good God, meaning the multi-skilled, and was prominent among the Tuatha de Danann. He carried a huge club that required more than eight men to lift it. One end was used for killing men and the other for restoring them to life. He also owned a magic harp whose music could unlock the seasons and on which he played the Three Noble Strains of Ireland, the glad-strain, the grief-strain and the sleep-strain. The Dagda also possessed a magic cauldron which yielded an abundance of food and had the power to revive life. Besides having a huge appetite for food, the Dagda also had a huge sexual appetite. He coupled with Boann of the River Boyne, fathering Aengus Og, the God of Love, and on the same day he also coupled with the Morrigan as she stood astride the River Unius.

Autumn, from Amergin's Poem to the Seasons

Autumn is the season for being indoors.
Before the days grow short there is work to be done.
Deer are abroad with their young, sheltered by the bracken,
and stags respond to the lowing of the hinds.
The woods are strewn with acorns,
the fields with stalks of corn.
Thorny bushes and brambles have overgrown the court
which lies in ruins. Ripe fruit rots on the hardened soil,
an abundance of hazel nuts falls from the sheltering trees.

FINN AND THE
SALMON OF WISDOM

When he was a boy, Finn was known as Demna. He was sent for instruction to an old druid called Finn the Seer. The seer was waiting by Fec's pool, on the River Boyne. Nine magical hazel trees surrounded the pool and dropped crimson hazelnuts into the water. Five salmon lived in the pool and fed from the hazelnuts. The seer knew that the salmon were imbued with inspirational knowledge and wisdom. He had been given a prophecy that one called Finn was destined to eat one of them and receive these gifts, so he waited day and night for the miracle to happen. Then one morning, he saw that a salmon had leaped out of the pool. He told the boy to go and cook it and bring it back to him. This the boy did, but on his return, the seer noticed a change in him.

"Did you eat any of the salmon?" he asked Demna.

"No," said the boy, "except that a blister rose up on it and I pressed it down with my thumb."

"Then it is to you that the Knowledge has come," said the other, "but I did not know your name was Finn."

The boy replied, "That is my nickname, because of my golden hair."

CORMAC'S CUP OF TRUTH

After Cormac had journeyed through the Land of Youth, he was entertained by a warrior and his wife. A feast was served and a golden cup was put into the hand of the warrior. Cormac looked at the cup, for it had curious carvings upon it.

"If this cup seems strange to you," said the warrior, "its property is even stranger. For if three false words are spoken under it, it will break into three pieces, but if three words of truth are spoken under it, it will be mended." Then the warrior spoke three falsehoods under the cup and immediately it broke into three. "It requires that you speak words of truth now," he said, "in order that the cup may be restored."

So Cormac said, "I can tell you that until today I have not set eyes on my wife, my son or my daughter since they were taken out of Tara by the youth on the green." At this the cup was made whole. After that his family were restored to him and he was given the cup to take to his own land. From that time it was called Cormac's Cup and was used to distinguish truth from falsehood.

THE DAMSELS OF THE WELLS

At one time the Land of Britain had many wells upon it and each well had a damsel in attendance who would offer water and refreshment to weary knights or travellers who passed that way. They offered food on dishes of silver and water in cups of gold. But the day came when King Amangans ruled the land and considered that he had a right to please himself however he chose. As he was riding one day with his men, he seized one of the maidens, raped her and stole her golden cup. Then his men followed suit, raping the damsels and stealing their costly cups and dishes. After that, throughout the land, the damsels disappeared from their wells, and without their attendance the waters dried up and the land became waste. It remained barren until the time when King Arthur and his knights set out to rescue the wells and reappoint the damsels. They found the descendants of the damsels imprisoned in the Castle of Maidens, and released them.

WHITE WILLOW

White willow, or *saille*, is closely linked to water and is usually found near rivers. It was an emblem of grief, its twigs being carried by mourners. In Greek myth Orpheus carried branches of willow into Hades when he went to seek Euridice. The Orphic mysteries concerned entering and returning from the Underworld and it is not surprising that the Celts, too, connected the willow with death. When bare, its form is gnarled and hag-like, but its leaves are white on the underside and, in summer, when rippled by the wind, they lend it sound and movement. A feminine tree, its groves were sacred to the Goddess. The willow was also linked with the moon and its power was particularly strong at night. That was the time when witches visited the trees and took their bark and leaves for spells and healing. Many feared the willow and some even believed that groups of willows could be seen walking at night. The tree was considered mystical by the Druids, who used it in their divinations. Its branches, being lithe and pliant, were woven into baskets and coracles.

White willow, saille, watery one
your shivering white-waved branches hide your form.
Soft-whispering muse of goddess groves,
and grieving garland are you. Talismanic guide
through death's strange shadowland.
Crouched is your shape, wrinkled and gnarled
Wise women work with you, peel off your bark
and crush your leaves to make their medicines.
Potent withy, moon-blanched witches' tree,
watchful, night-walking
Cailleach, visionary ...

NIALL OF THE NINE HOSTAGES

King Eochu of Ireland had four sons from his wife Mongfind, and a fifth, Niall, from a Saxon woman. To avoid the wrath of Mongfind, Niall was brought up away from the court by Torna the Poet. When he came of age, Niall returned to court and took his place beside his brothers in the contest for kingship. One day the five brothers were out hunting and became lost in the forest. Lighting a fire, they ate enough game to keep them from hunger, but they had no water. They found a well and one by one the brothers went to fill their cup from it. But the well was guarded by a hag so loathsome that each man quailed at the sight of her. The price for a cup of water, she declared, was to kiss her.

The four brothers declared they would rather die of thirst, but Niall consented and lay down with her. To his astonishment, in his arms her body became soft and fragrant, her eyes full and beautiful and her skin white as fresh-fallen snow. She had golden shoes on her feet and a purple cloak around her shoulders. Trembling, he asked who she was. "I am Sovereignty," she replied, "and in my hand is the gift of kingship."

THE WELL BY THE WAYSIDE

Orchards of Cenn Escrach,
pleasant home of the honey bee,
in the midst of you a gleaming spinney
with a wooden cup for drinking.

CUCHULAINN REJECTS THE MORRIGAN

When Cuchulainn was defending Ulster against Queen Medbh's army, a noble-looking woman approached him, wearing a dress of many colours. She said she had brought great wealth and cattle for him and had fallen in love with him because of his great prowess.

"You have come at the worst of times," said Cuchulainn, "for I am drained by war and have no thoughts of entertaining a woman."

"But what if I can help you?" she answered.

"I have more important considerations than the backside of a woman!" he retorted.

"If you refuse me," she said, "I will become an implacable enemy. While you are fighting I will come as an eel and wind around you and trip you up."

"Then I'll crush your ribs with my feet!'

"I'll come as a she-wolf and drive the wild beasts against you in the ford!"

"Then I'll take your eye out with my sling!"

"I'll become a red heifer and make the herd trample you in the water!"

"Then I'll break your leg with a stone!" said Cuchulainn. "And you will bear all these marks unless I lift them with a blessing!"

Then the woman went away. But Cuchulainn did not know that it was the Morrigan herself who had come to him.

THE CURSE OF MACHA

Crundchu, husband of the beautiful Macha, was attending the horse-racing at the Assembly of the Ultonians. He watched as two of the King's horses carried off every prize and boasted that his wife could outrun any horse in the land. Immediately the King demanded proof of this and Macha was sent for. When she arrived, all could see that she was close to childbirth. Macha begged the King to delay her trial until after she had given birth, but he threatened to kill Crundchu if she refused to run. Then she appealed to the crowd, adjuring them by their mothers not to insist on her trial at that time, but her request was denied. So Macha exerted all her strength and outran the horses, and afterwards fell to the ground, giving birth to twins.

Then she rose up in pain and exhaustion and cursed the men of Ulster. "From this time," she said, "whenever your power is needed in Ulster, you shall endure the pangs of childbirth. They will fall on you for five days and four nights unto the ninth generation." Then she died. After that, whenever the men of Ulster were needed to defend their province they were overcome by the Pangs of Macha.

The Horse of Command

The horse, or *each*, was the close companion of the Celtic warrior. It carried him across land, led him into battle, and pulled his chariot. Noble and faithful, it took on the soul of its master, even possessing intuitive knowledge about him. Cuchulainn's two horses, the Grey of Macha and the Black of Saingliu, were born at the same time as him, and at his last battle the Grey of Macha wept tears of blood, anticipat- ing his death. Although dark horses retained an ancient connection with death, white horses in particular were connected with the power and energy of the sun and the bright borderland of the Otherworld. By mastering such a powerful creature the Celt experienced the triumph of will over unruly forces. The horse therefore symbolised dignity and self-discipline. Women were also closely allied to horses. The horse-goddess Epona had a cult that swept through Gaul and Britain and she was even worshipped in Rome. Her Welsh equivalent was Rhiannon. Another such goddess was the Irish Macha, who was able to outrun the King's horses.

Tamed beast,
living chariot,
swift-flashing, fiery steed,
air-spirit, earthed.
Land-pounding traveller
to sun-specked meadows
of heroic feasting,
Macha ran with you,
Epona took your worship,
wronged Rhiannon
bowed her proud head
and gave your service.
Faithful blood-weeping
warrior, white-crested rider
of the ninth bright wave,
the Spirit threshold.

THE GODDESS AS SOVEREIGNTY

The Goddess was inextricably connected with the land, being the very embodiment of it. Flowerbride figures such as Blodeuwedd, Olwen and Guinevere give clear evidence of this. But there are also many tales of the Goddess appearing in her Crone aspect and testing the future king to see if he is worthy of her hand. The story of the testing of Niall by the hag of the well is one of them and a similar story is found in Arthurian legend. In this story Gawain agrees to marry the hideous Lady Raglan in order to save Arthur's life. Gawain is invited by the hag to kiss her on their wedding night, whereupon she transforms into a beautiful maiden. Here the sovereignty aspect is slightly displaced for it is Arthur's and not Gawain's kingship that is made secure. Nevertheless the rewards of kingship are evident in these stories.

By contrast, if a king treats his queen badly, this invariably leads to the destruction of the kingdom. After Mallolwch, King of Ireland, banishes his wife Branwen to the kitchens, Ireland is laid waste by the hosts of Britain, and the Cauldron of Regeneration is broken. To the Celts, crimes against the Great Mother were crimes against the earth itself.

The Hunt on Arran

On the day of Lughnasadh, Finn and his Fianna would go up to Arran for a month's hunting. Cailte made this poem in praise of the island.

Island of stags, ringed by the ocean,
giving sustenance to hosts,
turning the blue spears crimson.

Plenteous deer on its slopes,
berries on its branches,
icy, shivering streams
and acorns on its oaks.

Plentiful hounds of prey,
a wealth of blackberries,
sloes of the blackthorn,
deer under the oaks.

Purple lichen-covered cliffs,
smooth green fields,
grass-covered crags,
the sporting of fawns and trout.

Rich pastures and fat swine,
gardens fair to the eye
nuts swelling on hazel boughs,
and curraghs sailing past.

At the height of summer,
lovely beyond imagining the trout
in the streams, the seagulls
crying from the cliffs,
the fair island of Arran.

MAELDUN AND THE CAT

Maeldun and his men came to an island on which was a high fortress gleaming pale as snow in the evening light. They went ashore and entered the fortress, marvelling at the pure white houses inside. They went into the largest house. There was no sign of life, only a cat on a row of four pillars, jumping from one marble-capped column to another. The walls were lined with treasures—brooches, torcs, and swords of gold and silver. A boiled ox, a salt pig and a jug of clear ale were set out in the middle of the room. The men ate the meat and drank the ale. Afterwards they slept on feathered couches.

Next morning, they prepared to set sail and Maeldun's foster-brother asked if he could take one of the gold torcs. Maeldun warned him against taking anything for fear of angering the guardian of that place. Nevertheless the man picked up the largest torc. At once the cat hurled itself through the air and pierced his body like a flaming spear, reducing him to ashes. Maeldun quickly replaced the torc, speaking courteous words to the cat. Then he gathered up the ashes of his foster-brother, and they scattered them across the water as they rowed away.

THE HARP OF THE DAGDA

During the Second Battle of Mag Tuiread—fought between the Tuatha de Danann and the Fomorians, the Dagda's harper, Uaithne, was captured and the harp with him. Then the Dagda set out with his son Aengus Og to rescue it from the Fomorian banqueting hall. They entered the hall and found the enemy already feasting. At the far end the harp was hanging on the wall. The Dagda called to it:

> Come, Four-angled frame of harmony,
> Come, *Coir-cethair-chuir*!
> Come summer, come winter
> out of the mouths of harps and bags and pipes!

At once the harp came to his hand across the hall, killing nine men in its passage. Then the Dagda began to play on it. First he conjured the music of the grief-strain and those that were listening began to mourn and weep. Then he played the strain of happiness and all began laughing and rejoicing. Lastly he played the sleep-strain, so that all who heard it fell into a deep slumber. While they slept, the Dagda, Uaithne and Aengus Og made their escape unharmed.

The Three Feats of the Tuatha

Lugh, the Dagda, Ogma, Goibniu the smith and Diancécht the healer called a secret gathering of the Tuatha de Danann and asked how they should overcome the Fomorians. Mathgen the Sorcerer answered: "I will cause the twelve great mountains of Ireland to fall on them. The mountains will obey the bidding of the goddess Danu by falling with their heads to the earth and destroying the enemy around them."

Then the cup-bearer said: "I will command the twelve great lakes of Ireland to hide their water when the Fomorians come to them, but to yield water to the troops of the Tuatha. This shall be accomplished, though the war last for seven years."

Then Fingal the Druid said: "I shall cause fire to rain down upon the faces of the Fomorian warriors. I shall diminish their strength and courage. However, every breath the Tuatha take will embolden them and they will never become fatigued, even if the war should last seven years."

After that the Dagda spoke saying: "All these feats offered by the sorcerer, the cup-bearer and the druid, I can achieve alone."

AUTUMN

After the delight of summer
in each field and hollow
comes the weeping of the leaves,
the long sorrow.

THE WISDOM OF THE OAK

King of trees, the oak was especially sacred to the Druids, who performed their rites within its groves. It is the most long-lived tree apart from the yew. Strong and solid, it became an emblem of perseverance and stability. Linked to the sun and with lightning, it was believed to have oracular powers. At Lughnasadh it is able to produce new shoots which revive its glory. Connected with the sun, it was believed to battle the holly at midsummer and wrest back its kingly crown. It was the habitation of the oak-god, Herne the Hunter.

> *Duir*, tree of the Druids,
> gnarled, deep-rooted. In your bark
> runs healing, in your branches
> prophecy. Subject to lightning
> and the god of sky, you speak
> men's fortunes. Long-lived
> haunt of Herne, empowered by sun,
> strength-giver, constant, wise,
> keeper of ancient knowledge,
> druids took your name
> and made your holy, shaded groves
> their temples.

BREHONS

Brehons were Druidic judges. They compiled an ancient legal code, the Brehon Laws, which later became the system of Irish law known as the *Seanchus Mor*. These contained, for example, laws against violence and laws enforcing compassionate treatment of the sick. They also contained many references to the use of the Ogham script. Ogham symbols were cut into standing stones to denote ownership of land.

The Brehons travelled throughout the country, presiding over disputes and setting punishments. Their most severe sentence was an ancient form of excommunication, that of banning a tribe or individual from participating in a ritual sacrifice to the gods. Such punishment was greatly feared, because it barred entry into the Otherworld at death. Besides using their secular authority, Brehons also used their shamanic and divinatory skills to settle issues. They were often able to reveal the truth through their powers of psychometry and spontaneous verse-making.

Ceridwen and the Cauldron of Awen

Ceridwen prepared her cauldron with herbs and with bones of creatures of the dark and with spices and incantations and with all that should give knowledge, wisdom and inspiration to her son Avagddu. Then she set the boy Gwion Bach to stir it. And Gwion stirred the cauldron for a year and a day. But on the last day of the stirring what should happen but three drops should jump out of the brew and land on his thumb, throbbing there like three burning seeds. Quicker than thought he put his finger to his mouth to soothe it. But as fate would have it, these were the three drops that contained within them all the virtue of the brew: the drop of knowledge, the drop of wisdom and the drop of inspiration.

When Gwion Bach had sucked his thumb he was suddenly filled with the knowledge of everything in the whole world. But the first thing he knew was that Ceridwen herself would come after him in a deadly rage, intending to kill him. So he took to his heels and ran away with the speed of the wind.

Autumn Equinox

21 September

Festival of equal balance, night with day, and dark with light. Day of the sun-god poised in the heavens before his slow descent. Last day of the reign of light. Time of completion, fullness, ending. Feast of the goddess, grain-giver and gift- bearer, holder of the *herfest*, store of richness, overflowing cornucopia. Hail to you wise Mother, with your womb of fullness, sacrificial Sovereign of the land. Hail to the young son, the Mabon, prince of light, star in the darkness, harbinger of hope. Now is the waning of the sun, the time of waiting, time of storing grain in vaults of darkness. Hail to Ceridwen, harvest-goddess, Mother of the bard and mystical inspirer. Hail to the cauldron's gifts of hidden wisdom, knowledge, intuition. Welcome to the resting time, the inner sleeping, time when the buried powers begin their secret working.

THE THREE INNER CAULDRONS

In Celtic lore there were believed to be three mystical cauldrons inside each human being. The first, the Cauldron of Warming, lay upright in the belly and provided inner warming and bodily nourishment. The second, the Cauldron of Vocation, lay on its side within the heart, and quivered at its emotions. In extreme joy or sorrow it could tip over, becoming a gift-giving vessel of discernment and nobility, strength and eloquence. The third was the Cauldron of Knowing, which was upside down and located in the head, the seat of spirit and inspiration. But only the wise ones, the Druids, the possessors of *awen*, knew the power of this cauldron turned upwards. Then it became the giver of inspiration and Otherworldly knowledge, the vessel of spiritual insight, truth and poetic utterance.

Dafydd ap Gwilym Laments the Death of his Patron

The court of Ifor Hael
lies in the arms of alders.
Thorns and bracken hold
where once was song and feasting.

No bards or poets spin their tales,
no laden tables stand,
no gold or precious prizes,
no gift-giving lord.

For Dafydd, the silver-tongued,
bitter it was to lay his lord in clay.
Now the ancient song-paths
are empty and owl-haunted.

Rich once and now laid low,
the great lords in their halls
how swiftly their former pride
falls into dust and ruin.

The Salmon of Wisdom

The salmon, or *Bradan*, is an extraordinary fish, being equally at home in salt or fresh water. It also demonstrates powers of endurance and sacrifice, swimming long distances upriver in order to spawn, after which it dies. A creature of the water, it is an ancient inhabitant of the feminine realm of inspiration and mysticism. In the account of the Seeking of the Mabon in the story of Culhwch and Olwen, the Salmon of Llyn Llyw is depicted as the oldest creature and the only one who knows where the Mabon, or sacred child, can be found. The symbolism of the sacred salmon and its link with Inspiration and Wisdom is central to Celtic spirituality. The Celts believed the source of Otherworldly knowledge was found in the Well of Wisdom, which was surrounded by nine hazel trees of Inspiration. Five sacred salmon lurked in its depths, feeding on the hazelnuts as they dropped into the well. Eating these salmon conferred prophetic insight and wisdom.

Cathbad Prophesies the Fate of Deirdre

When the wife of Felim, son of Daill, was nine months' pregnant, there came from her womb in the full hearing of King Conchobor and all his men, a fearful scream which echoed round the hall and chilled the hearts of all within it. Trembling the woman ran to Cathbad. The wise druid laid his hand upon her belly while the child struggled and stormed within it. Then he lifted up his voice and prophesied:

> There is in your womb, a girl, a woman.
> Her hair runs down her back like golden foam
> her cheeks are soft as foxgloves and her teeth
> white as the sun-struck snow, her eyes
> grey-pupilled and her lips bright crimson.
> She is destined to bring death to many heroes,
> therefore I name her Deirdre.

Then the men rose up and vowed to kill the child as soon as it was born, but Conchobor held up his hand and stopped them, saying he would marry her himself when she was come of age. Until that time he ordered that the child be kept from male company and brought up out of sight beyond the palace wall. And there she stayed, with only women round her and knowing only two men, her tutor Cailcin, and King Conchobor.

SACRED NUMBERS—THREE

The number three was a highly spiritual number and particularly sacred to the Celts. It was the number of the Goddess, who was triple-aspected as maiden, mother and crone. This mystical concept of "three-in-one" was carried forward into Christian belief. In Celtic myth, the number three was tripled to nine to denote magical groups of Otherworldly women. For example, the undersea island which King Ruadh visited was inhabited by nine women; the story of *Peredur* includes nine hags with whom King Arthur had to contend; and, in the *Preiddeu Annwn*, there is an account of nine women whose breath warmed the pearl-rimmed Cauldron of Regeneration. It is not surprising to find that the "ninth wave" is also important in Celtic mythology. It was beyond the ninth wave that the known world ended and the Otherworld began. Nine was also the number of inspiration, there being nine hazel-trees of inspiration fringing the Well of Wisdom.

The Secrets of the Seal, or *Selchie*

A creature of the water, the seal inhabits the depths of the unconscious and has been woven into legend. Tales of selchies or seal-men coming ashore and fathering children on mortal women are of ancient origin, and there are still those who believe that if a child has webbed hands or feet it is descended from a selchie.

In the Scottish tale of the Great Selchie of Sule Skerrie, the alluring seal-man marries a woman who conceives his child, but afterwards he leaves his wife and son and returns to the sea. Later he mysteriously reappears to claim the child. There is also a tale of a seal-woman who removes her skin to become human for a while but is captured by a fisherman who hides it and makes her his wife. Without her skin she loses touch with her inner nature. When, years later, she finds it again, she is able to regain her seal-shape and return to the sea. The seal symbolises the secret inner life and the emotions. Working with it enhances the powers of intuition and the link with feminine energies.

FLOOD-TIDE

See the great and glorious ocean in the north-east
dwelling of creatures, home of the seal,
full-wombed and magnificent,
it swells with the flood-tide.

THE FLOODING OF YS

After the city of Ys was built, Dahut lived in her castle and entertained suitors from far and wide with feasting and dancing. If she liked a suitor, she would have him brought secretly to her chamber. But after he had pleased her, he would be killed, and his body thrown into the waters below the castle.

One day a strange man arrived, dressed in red. When they had feasted, Dahut invited him to her chamber, but he refused to make love to her until she agreed to his request. He asked her for the key to the dyke and Dahut gave it to him. Then he went out and unlocked the floodgates. Immediately the sea rushed in and began engulfing the city.

As the waters rose, King Gradlon struggled to escape on horseback with Dahut clinging on behind him. Suddenly the abbot Guénolé called out and commanded him to thrust his daughter off the horse. When the King refused, the Abbot pushed her off with his staff. Immediately the King's horse sprang away, taking him to safe ground, while Dahut disappeared under the waves. Her fine city sank to the bottom of the sea and it is said that ever afterwards her voice could be heard, wailing and lamenting beneath the waters.

ASH—THE WORLD TREE

The ash, or *nuin*, was one of the most important trees for the Celts. Three great ash trees are cited along with the oak and the yew in the Five Magic Trees of Ireland. The season of the ash is brief, it is late to come to leaf and then loses its leaves early. It also exhausts the soil around it. Its wood is very hard and was used by the Celts to make spears. It was believed to have affinities with both the sun and the moon, and is regarded as significant in many mythologies. It is especially famous as Ygdrassil, the World Tree in Norse Myth, in which it is depicted with a serpent coiled round its base and an eagle resting in its crown. The serpent is an ancient symbol of feminine energies and connects it with the earth, while the eagle links it with the sun. All trees were believed to connect past and present, earth and sky, death and rebirth, female and male energies, but the ash was especially chosen to bring out these connections. It is on the world tree that the divine hero of myth is hanged and on the world tree that he is later revived. In Celtic myth Lleu Llaw Gyffes was turned into an eagle at death, and was found by Gwydion on top of the World Tree, and brought back to life and human form through the sacred power of poetry.

Spear-hard *Nuin*, Great World Tree
stretching out your arms to hold the sky
and reaching with your roots
into the deep black soil of ancient wisdom.
Silver-grey you stand
spinning your winged fruit,
waiting through the seasons,
pulling the strength of moon,
the light of sun. The wise old serpent
guards you, while the eagle waits
in your topmost branches.
Death's ritual is enacted on you
for you know its secret.
Thrice-named magic tree,
earth's deepest energies
rise to meet the sky-god
in your sacred pillar.

GRADLON'S CHOICE

After his darkly beautiful daughter Dahut was drowned, King Gradlon was taken to the Monastery of Landevennec by the abbot Guénolé. But the king said he could not stay so near the sea because he could hear the moaning and crying of his daughter, carried to him on the wind. So he went inland to the forest of Kranou and lived with a druid. The Abbot came to find him and begged him to return to the monastery, but Gradlon was dying and said he would rather remain with the druid. Then he begged Guénolé to respect the old man saying: "Do not be unkind to him, for, though I have lost my city and my daughter, the man is mourning the death of his gods and the end of his religion, which is the greatest pain of all."

Symbolic Colours—Gold

Perfect metal, flesh of gods and sacred fire of divinity. Glittering, transcendent, flowing from the sun. Wrested from darkness, hard-caught in the chasms of the Mother, you arise, light-bringing, radiant, pure. Heroes ride out to battle in your brilliance, sun-flashing golden torcs, neck-jewels, armlets, shields. Highest and most pleasing offering to the gods are you. A rich-wrought goblet dropped in the lake will confer great honour and appease an angry deity. Essence of knowledge is in you, shining Spirit-bearer. In you the *sidhe* delight, dining upon your dishes, drinking from your cups. The High King clothes his table with your beauty, courtiers raise your goblets in the flame-light. Rare, untarnished one of Otherworldly nature. Light-wielding, holder of hidden wisdom. Pathway of the sun, perfection's promise.

The Power of the *Englyn*

After Gwydion followed the sow to the World Tree, he looked up to see what she was feeding on. High in the topmost branch he saw an eagle, so badly wounded that his flesh was falling from him. Gwydion guessed that this was Lleu, so he summoned his greatest art and composed an *englyn*, a magic verse which alone might have the power to entice the spirit of Lleu down from the tree. This is what he sang:

> Oak that grows between two lakes,
> darkness over hill and sky,
> if it be true I speak no lie
> this flesh is from the wounds of Lleu.

At this the eagle descended to the middle of the tree, whereupon Gwydion sang another englyn:

> Oak that grows on woodland plain
> harmed by neither sun nor rain
> nine score tempests it endured,
> it bears the wounded form of Lleu.

At this the eagle descended to the lowest branch of the tree and Gwydion sang another englyn:

> Oak that grows upon a slope
> resting place of king or prince
> Shall I not compose a truth
> that Lleu will come into my lap.

At this the eagle dropped into his lap. Immediately Gwydion struck him with his wand, returning him to human form. But the man he cradled on his lap was skin and bone, barely alive.

FINN LEARNS THE TRUTH
THROUGH DIVINATION

After his hounds had fought in the hall and the child was found dead among them, Finn offered to give a fine, or *eric*, for the boy if it could be shown that the hounds had laid tooth or claw upon him. The child was examined and no mark of tooth or nail was found anywhere on his body. Then the boy's father, Roc, the steward of Aengus Og, put a fearful *geis* on Finn to divine who had killed his son. Finn asked for a *fidchell* board and some water. Then he washed his hands and put his thumb under his tooth whereupon the true knowledge came to him. And it was this: that Donn, the father of Diarmuid O'Duibna, had killed the boy by squeezing him between his knees.

Then Roc got a druid's wand and raised it over his son, transforming him into a wild boar, earless and tailless, telling the creature: "I put this fate upon you, that you bear the life of Diarmuid, that you and he meet your death together." At this the boar fled from the hall and went to the mountain of Ben Bulben. There he lived out his life, waiting for his own and Diarmuid's time to come.

Cuchulainn Heals the Morrigan

Because he refused her love, the Morrigan came against Cuchulainn in the shape of an eel, a she-wolf and a red heifer, but he overcame her in the ways that he had sworn. He crushed her ribs, took out her eye and shattered her leg, nor could these injuries be lifted from her without his blessing. Then she appeared to him as a cross-eyed hag milking a cow with three teats. When he asked for a drink, she gave him milk from one of the teats. "Blessing on you, Old Woman!" said Cuchulainn. At this her rib was restored. Then she gave him a drink from the second teat. "A blessing on you!" he said again, at which her eye was restored.

She gave him a drink from the last teat and, this time, her leg was made whole again. "You swore you would never lift these marks from me," said the Morrigan.

Cuchulainn replied, "Had I known who it was I would not have healed you!"

THE SOUL-QUALITY OF THE SWAN

The swan, or *eala*, symbolises love, beauty and inspiration. Throughout mythology there are stories of maidens transforming into swans and swans into maidens. Aengus Og, the god of love, falls in love with such a maiden. This magical transformation into the feminine also speaks of the link between the swan and the soul. The swan is also connected with water, purity, and death. In Irish myth the four Children of Lyr are turned into swans by their jealous stepmother. They are condemned to live first on one lake, then another, until nine hundred years have passed. They do, however, retain their voices and possess the power of song. The singing of the swan in mythology is particularly magical and denotes their Otherworldly nature.

White cloud on water,
light-shifting, delicate,
black-beaked with lifted wings,
arch-necked and proud. Soul's
sacred image, song-rich
messenger of love,
and Otherworldly
longing.

THE FATE OF THE CHILDREN OF LIR

Lir, of the Tuatha de Danann, had four children, two daughters named Finola and Aed and two sons, Fiacra and Conn. He loved these children dearly and after his wife died, they were a great consolation to him. But then he married again, and their foster-mother became very jealous of them, because of the love their father bore them. One day she drove them in her chariot to the Lake of Darvra and told them to go bathing. As soon as they were in the water, she took out a wand and struck each of them with it, turning them into four white swans.

Then she said: "I lay this enchantment on you, that you shall retain these shapes and dwell on this lake for three hundred years, and after that for a further three hundred years on the Sea of Moyle and after that, three hundred years on the Western Sea itself. But in that time you may keep your own speech and you shall have the power of song. Sweet, plaintive, faerie music you shall sing, which shall soothe mortals to sleep. And you shall keep your human reason, though you have the hearts and bodies of wild swans."

The Death of Diarmuid

One morning Diarmuid awoke and found that Finn and the Fianna had already gone out hunting. He went out and found Finn on the Mountain of Ben Bulben. Finn told him to go home, for they were hunting the wild boar and Diarmuid was under *geis* not to hunt it. But Diarmuid was determined to face the boar so Finn left him on the mountainside. Immediately the great boar came charging towards Diarmuid, who threw his spear at it. Undaunted the boar rushed on him and gashed his side open with its tusk. At the same time Diarmuid drove his sword through its brain. The boar fell dead, but Diarmuid had received a mortal wound.

As he lay there, Finn came up and Diarmuid begged him to bring water and heal him, for Finn had this power. So Finn went to a spring and filled his hands with water, but when he reached Diarmuid, he thought of Grainne, and such was his jealousy that he let the water trickle away. He went to the spring a second time, but again let the water spill on the ground. A third time he went and this time poured the water over Diarmuid's wound, healing it. But it was too late, for Diarmuid was already dead.

ALDER—THE BLEEDING TREE

The alder, or *fearn*, like the willow, grows beside streams and rivers. It needs boggy terrain in order to survive and propagate. A small tree, graceful and slender, its wood is extremely hard. It resists decay in water and is used for making bridges, jetties and underwater pillars. It also burns at a high temperature and was used by smiths. It was particularly sacred to the Druids because when cut its sap runs white and then turns pinkish red; hence it was known as the Bleeding Tree. It is likely that alder groves were used in rituals and their trunks slashed to produce magical empathetic bleeding. The red sap also produced a dye called roeim which Celtic warriors painted on their faces when going into battle. Whistles and pipes were made from alder branches, and were used by druids to call up elemental winds and spirits. Because of its musical pipes, the crown of the alder tree was sometimes called the "oracular singing head."

Fearn, alder, slender dancing tree
drawing on streams and rivers for your energies.
When cut by men you bleed,
when burned your flame is fierce
blazing the fires of smiths to forge their weaponry.
Men wear your staining on their face
in battle. With your whistles
druids call their airy elementals,
witches shrill their storms. Sweet
incense rising from your branches
summons gods. Your wind-blown harmonies
crown you the Singing Head of Bran.
Beguiling, fiery, spindle-wanded one
sap-dripping in your groves
a wounded empathy.

Aengus Converses with Diarmuid

After Diarmuid was killed by the Boar of Ben Bulben, Aengus Og, the god of love, ordered that Diarmuid's body be born to his palace at the Brug on the Boyne. So his body was brought on its golden bier with Diarmuid's own spears and javelins raised over it and pointing upwards. There, at the Brug na Boyne, Aengus mourned his foster-son lamenting that for the one night of his life that he had not kept watch over him, Diarmuid had been killed by the treachery of Finn. He sang these words over him:

> Alas, sweet Diarmuid with the glowing face,
> bold warrior, chief in courage among the Fianna
> Fair one of the white teeth,
> conqueror of the hearts of women,
> the treachery of Finn has overcome you.
>
> Alas, sweet Diarmuid,
> the life flows from you
> poison has entered you,
> the fierce wild boar
> has triumphed and laid you low,
> Diarmuid of the shining weapons.

Then Aengus, being unable to restore him to life, sent a soul into him so that he and Diarmuid were able to talk together for a little while each day.

SACRED SYMBOLS—THE CELTIC CROSS

The cross is one of the most ancient of all symbols. Its vertical line represents the spiritual dimension and is a type of world-axis linking heaven and earth, while its horizontal arm represents the earth and mankind. The point at which they meet is the union of heaven and earth, spirit and flesh, god and creation. The cross itself is a well-known and widespread symbol, but the Celtic cross is unique in that it encloses the cross in a circle. The circle represents the turning wheel of the seasons, the cycle of manifestations, and the solar deity. Enclosing the cross within the circle, therefore, gave it a more holistic significance.

The Celts were aware of the importance of the centrepoint of the cross and often enclosed that, again, within a smaller circle. Thus the Celtic cross combined three symbols: the two-arms of the cross, the circle of divinity, and the centre-point—the meeting between heaven and earth. The concept of the cross within the circle was also used in the Celtic swastika symbol, where it represented the turning wheel of the sun. The short branches, set at right-angles to the four arms, were often curved and bending in a clockwise direction, demonstrating the solar circuit.

OISIN RETURNS FROM
THE LAND OF YOUTH

When Oisin had spent some years in the Land of Youth, feelings for his old land and his former companions began to stir in him. "I wish to visit my homeland," he said. Niamh replied, "It would be better if you did not go, for you will find it much changed." But Oisin insisted. So Niamh lent him her white horse but begged him not to let his feet touch the ground.

The horse took him across the water, past islands and marvels until he came to the shores of Ireland. He went to the Hill of Allen and was astonished at the small size of the people. He asked an old woman for news of the Fianna. She said he spoke of heroes long gone. Then he found the great hall lying deserted, its walls overgrown with weeds and bushes. Horror came on him and he stretched out his arms, shouting into the silence for Finn and the other warriors. Then he saw a group of men straining to roll aside a boulder. He leaned over and pushed the boulder down the hill, but as he did so, his saddle-girth broke, pitching him to the ground. As soon as he touched the ground, three hundred years came upon him and he turned into a wizened old man.

Remembrances on the Hill of Howth

How lovely the Hill of Howth
place of perfection, poised above milky waves,
a sea of gulls. Blessed are you,
sweet, fierce vine-grown peak.

The peak of Howth, the haunt of Finn
and the brave-hearted Fianna,
cups and drinking-horns were here.
Here, too, brave Diarmuid brought Grainne
with hot-hearted Finn pursuing them.

Lovely peak, soaring above all others,
craggy, ringed with green
beast-haunted, wooded, wild,
bristling with swordsmen,
scented with wild garlic,
sporting trees of many hues.

Fairest in the land of Ireland are you,
O peak of brightness, hovering above
a waving sea of white birds,
it is no small thing for me to leave
the beautiful Hill of Howth.

THE BRIGHT AND FLOURISHING SPRING

When they came to the top of the Hill of Usnagh, Diarmait, the King of Ireland conceived a great thirst, but was told there was no water in that place. Then Oisin asked for a basin and set out alone to look for water. But he cast a spell of invisibility over himself so that no one should see where he went. He was looking for the Spring of Usnagh, known as the bright and flourishing spring, which had not been seen for many years. But Oisin found it and knelt on its stony bed. He saw eight beautiful speckled salmon swimming in its waters and caught them in his basin. He covered them with eight sprigs of watercress and brooklime, and carried them back to King Diarmait.

The King said the salmon should be divided between himself and Patrick, but Patrick said the king should have the greater part because his retinue was greater. "Let the Church take a third, for that is its due," he said, "and let the High King have two thirds." And this was done. But Patrick cautioned Oisin against laying too much store on the salmon in case he should imperil his soul.

The Spring

Leaping spring of Tráigh Dhá Bhan
fair are you covered in cress, untended.
Place where brook-lime no longer grows,
trout on your banks, wild pigs
haunting your wilderness.
Stags and red dapple-breasted fawns are on your crag,
nuts hang on your tree-tops,
fish breast the waters of your streams.
Beautiful is the colour of your lilies on their tender stems,
green spring flowing in the leafy combe.

Dialogue Between
St. Patrick and Oisin

OISIN: How could it be that God and his priests are better men than Finn, and he so generous and without blemish? Woeful is the tale that says Finn is kept in bonds!

PATRICK: Let us not quarrel any more, you withered old man who has lost all sense! Know this, that God is in his high heaven and Finn and the Fianna dwell in the place of pain.

OISIN: Great, then, is the shame of God, if he refuses to release Finn from such shackles. For if God himself were in pain or any difficulty, Finn would redeem him with silver or gold, or through fighting and battle, until he was victorious! And moreover, it is shame on your God that I sit here among his priests and am denied food, clothing or music, with no recompense for my bardic skills, no hunting, battling or courting beautiful women, no sport, no seat of honour and no trials of agility.

THE ANGELS' INSTRUCTIONS

In the time when St. Patrick came to Ireland and began preaching Christianity, it is said that two of the old Fenians, Cailte and Oisin, though very ancient, were still living. One day Cailte visited the Fortress of the Red Bridge where Patrick was staying, and the Fenian was of such stature that the monks reached only to his waist. Then Patrick asked him about Finn and the deeds of the Fianna. Cailte began to tell him the tales until Patrick said that in listening to him he was neglecting his prayers and offices.

Then Patrick went to pray, and his two guardian angels, Aibelán and Solusbrethach, came to him. He asked them if it was Christ's will that he listen to the tales of the Fianna. The angels answered in one voice, "Dear holy man, these warriors can only tell you a third of their stories, for that is all they can remember. But command that these stories be written down on poets' tablets so that hearing them may give joy and gladness to those who come in later times."

Three Candles that Illumine Every Darkness

Truth
Nature
Knowledge

GLOSSARY AND PRONUNCIATION GUIDE

As a general guide to Welsh pronunciation, *ll* sounds *cl* or *chl*; *dd* sounds *th*, as in "then" (represented below as *dh*); *ch* and *gh* are guttural.

In Irish pronunciation *b* sounds *v*; *c* sounds *g* or *k*; *ch* is guttural, *d* sounds *th*, as in "then" (represented below as *dh*); *g* is a soft gutteral and sounds *gh*; *m* sounds *v*; *t* sounds *d*. An *s* with either *i* or *e* before or after it is pronounded *sh*; *th* is pronouned softly as in "thin"; *ai* is pronounced as *a*; *ei* is pronounced as *e*.

Aengus *Angus*—son of Boann and the Dagda. God of Love
Ailill *Alil*—King of Connaught and husband of Queen Medbh
Ainnli Brother of Naoise
Amargin *Avarghin*—poet-seer; leader of the Milesians
Annwn *Anoon*—the Celtic Underworld or Otherworld
Arianrhod Arianrod—sister of Gwydion, mother of Lleu Llaw Gyffes
Avagddu *Av-ugdhi*—misshapen son of Welsh goddess Ceridwen

Badbh *Badhv*—one of the triple war goddesses
Banba One of the triple goddesses of Ireland
Bedwyr Celtic name for Sir Bedivere of Arthurian legend
Beli Legendary ancient British king
Beltain Festival around 1 May

Blodeuwedd *Blod-eye-wedh*—wife made out of flowers for Lleu

Boann Mother of Aengus mac Og, gave name to the River Boyne

Bran Known as Bran the Blessed, ruled Britain from Harlech; brother of Branwen; his severed head became oracular

Bricriu Known as "the Poison-tongued," Ulster hero, mischief-maker

Brighid *Bridge-id*—goddess of smithcraft, inspiration and healing

Brug, Brugh *Brew*—Aengus' palace beside the River Boyne

Cailleach *Kailyak*—Crone aspect of the Goddess

Cailte *Kweeltya*—one of the last surviving Fenians

Cantref *Kantrev*—Welsh unit of land, a hundred homesteads

Carpre Irish bard whose satire raised boils on the face of King Bres

Cathbad *Kathvadh*—Chief Druid to King Conchobor of Ulster

Cet *Ket*—a Connaught warrior

Cian Earthly father of Lugh; killed by Sons of Tuirenn

Conchobar *Kon-ch-ovar*—King of Ulster c. beginning Christian era

Connaught Western province of Ireland, ruled by Medbh and Ailill

Connle Irish prince who falls in love with faerie woman and is lured to the Land of Youth

Cormac mac Art King, 227–266 CE

Cruachu *Kruakoo*—royal seat of Medbh and Ailill in Connaught; also site of cave entrance to Otherworld

Crundchu Wealthy Irish herdsman, marries Macha

Cuchulainn *Ku-chull-in*—"Hound of Culann"; hero of Ulster cycle

Culhwch *Kullhukh*—cousin of King Arthur, woos Olwen

Dafydd ap Gwilym *Davith ap Gwilim*—Welsh bard c. 1325–1380

Dagda   Chief god of the Tuatha de Danann

Dahut   *Da-hoot*—daughter of Gradlon, a Breton king

Deirdre   Daughter of Felim, Conchobor's storyteller, eloped with Ulster warrior Naoise

Demna   Original name of Finn mac Cumhail

Diarmuid   *Dermot*—grandson of Duibne (Dina), Fenian warrior abductor of Grainne.

Emain   *Macha Evin Ma-cha*—capital of Ulster

Emer   *Ay-ver*—wife of Cuchulainn

Eoghan   *Yo-gh-an*—King of Farney, a dependant of Conchobar

Etain   Faerie woman loved by Midhir

Ferchetne   Ferketny—chief poet of Conchobar

Fergus mac Roich   *Fergus mac Ro-eh*—great Ulster hero, one-time King of Ulster, defected to Connaught after Sons of Usna were killed

Fianna   Organised military band led by Finn mac Cumhail

Fidchell   *Fi-kell*—board game similar to chess

Fili   *Feely*—Irish poet-seer

Findabhair   *Findavir*—daughter of Medbh and Ailill

Finn (Fionn) mac Cumhail   Fyun m' Cool—Captain of the Fianna

Froech   Froeekh—son of Boann

Geis   *Gaysh*—magical taboo or prohibition

Goll mac Morna   "Blind son of Morna" one-eyed rival of Finn, slayer of Finn's father

Grainne   *Graun-yeh*—daughter of Cormac mac Art, wife of Finn elopes with Diarmuid

Gwalchmei   *Gwalkmai*—Celtic name of Gawain of Arthurian legend

Gwydion   Magician uncle of Lleu, for whom he and Math magically make a bride, Blodeuwedd

Gwynedd   *Gweh-nedh*—district of north-west Wales

Imbolc   Festival, around 1 February (also called Oimelc)

Iseult   *Eesolt*—wife of King Mark of Cornwall, elopes with Trystan

Kei   *Kye*—knight of King Arthur

Levarcham   *Leevarham*—woman satirist, messenger of Conchobar, guardian of Deirdre

Lir or **Ler**   Sea-god, father of Manannan

Lleu Llaw Gyffes   *Chlay Chlow Geh-feth*—magically birthed son of Arianrhod

Lludd   *Lud (or Chludh)*—ancient king of Britain

Lugh   *Loo*—son of the Dagda, a chief of the Tuatha, god of light, father of Cuchulainn

Lughnasadh   *Loonassa*—harvest festival associated with Lugh

Macha   *Ma-kha*—faerie woman, wife of Crundchu

Maeldun   Legendary captain of crew of seafarers

Mag Tuiread   *Maytura*—Site of battle between the Tuatha and the Famorians

Mallolwch   *Mallollokh*—King of Ireland

Manannan   Sea-god, a chief of the Tuatha de Danann

Math   King of Gwynedd, uncle of Gwydion

Medbh   *Madhv or Mave*—Queen of Connaught

Midhir   *Mithir*—a lord of the faerie people

Morrigan Goddess of war

Naoise   *Noy-shee*—Son of Usna, eloped with Deirdre

Niall   Known as "of the Nine Hostages'; historical Irish king, established fifth province and capital at Tara

Niamh   *Neeve*—faerie woman who lured Oisin to Otherworld

Nuada   First king of Tuatha; lost hand in battle, had a silver one made for him.

Ogham   *O'am*—cryptic Druidic language

Oisin   *Osheen*—Fenian warrior, son of Finn

Olwen   Daughter of ogre Ysbaddaden; wooed by Cullwch

Preiddeu Annwn   *Priddy Anoon*—account of Arthur's raid on Otherworld

Pwyll   *Poochl*—with *oo* as in "foot"—Lord of Dyfed who changed places with Arawn, Lord of Annwn

Rath   Fortified dwelling surrounded by wall or ditch

Red Branch   Name of assembly Hall at Emain and of Ulster warrior band

Ruadh *Ruad*—King of Scotland

Samhain *Sowain*—festival marking start of Celtic year; origin of Hallowe'en

Scathach *Scaw-thach*—female warrior who trained Cuchulainn

Sidhe *Shee*—faerie, also burial mound or barrow

Slieve A mountain, or mountainous district

Tailtiu Mother of Lugh, daughter of King of Spain

Tain Bo Cuailnge *Toyn Bo Cooling*—the Cattle Raid of Cooley, central epic of Ulster Cycle

Taliesin Greatest bard of Wales

Tara Seat of High Kings of Ireland in County Meath.

Tir na n'Og *Teer nan Owg*—the Land of Youth, or Otherworld

Tristan Nephew of King Mark and lover of Iseult in Arthurian legend

Tuatha de Danann *Tooatha day Daanan*—race that conquered Ireland and later dwelt in the faerie mounds

Uaithne *Ooaythnie*—harper to the Dagda

Usna *Oozna* (with *oo* as in "foot')

Ygdrasil *Eegdrasil*—the World Tree in Norse myth

Ys *Ees*—mythical city in Brittany

Ysbaddaden *Ees-badh-aden*—ogre father of Olwen

Sources and Resources

Bibliography

Aubert, O. L. Aubert, *Celtic Legends of Brittany*, Coop Breizh (Kerangwenn) 1993

Dooley, A. and Row, H. (trans), *Tales of the Elders of Ireland*, OUP 1999

Gantz, Jeffrey (trans.), *The Mabinogion*, Penguin 1976

Hyde, Douglas, *A Literary History of Ireland*, T. Fisher Unwin 1899

Jackson, Kenneth Hurlstone (trans.), *A Celtic Miscellany*, Penguin 1971

Kinsella, Thomas (trans.) *The Tain*, OUP 1969

Matthews, Caitlin and John, *The Encyclopaedia of Celtic Wisdom*, Rider 2001

Monmouth, Geoffrey of, *The History of the Kings of Britain* (trans. Lewis Thorpe), Penguin 1966

Paterson, Jacqueline Memory, *Tree Wisdom*, Thorsons 1996

Rolleston, T. W., *Celtic Myths and Legends*, Senate 1994

Many of the poems in this book are the author's reworkings of ancient Celtic poems and descriptions which are still in existence. A list of these is given below. All other poems are the original creations of the author, and are inspired by her many years of working within the bardic tradition.

Aengus' Lament for Diarmuid

Amergin's Poems of the Seasons

Autumn

Black is the Lake

Cathbad's Prophecy concerning Deirdre

Cold is the Night

The Counsel of Finn

Dafydd ap Gwilym Laments the Death of his Patron

Deirdre Remembering a Scottish glen

Etain

Etain Becomes a Butterfly

A Faerie House

Flood-tide

Froech in the Dark Pool

The Generosity of Finn

The Generosity of the Sidhe

Gwydion's Englyn

The Harp of the Dagda

The Harp

The Hunt on Arran

Invitation from the Lord of the Faeries

Iseult's poem on evergreen trees

The Island of Albion

Lament for the Poet Mael Mhuru

May-Time

The Monk's Mistress
The Oath of the Elements
Olwen
Oran's Revelation
The Power of the Word (Nede's lines)
Remembrances on the Hill of Howth
Slieve Gua
The Song of Amergin
The Song of the Blackbird
The Splendour of King Cormac
The Spring
The Well by the Wayside
Welsh triads
Winter
Winter Cold
A Wretched Life

Discography

Noirin Ni Riain, *Celtic Soul*, Earth Music Productions, LMUS 0031

Loreena McKennitt, *Parallel Dreams*, Quinlan Road Ltd, Canada, QRCD 103

Celtic Woman (compilation), Celtic Woman Records, CWRCD 7001

Alan Stivell, *Renaissance of the Celtic Harp*, Rounder Records, Massachusetts, CD 3067

Available from C. Hamilton, c/o the publisher, or at:
        claire@clairehamilton. com:
Company of Strangers, *Blodeuwedd—A Wife out of Flowers*, COS 298
Company of Strangers, *The Love-Song of Diarmuid and Grainne*, CSSM1
        (cassette)
The Celtic Harp, Sound and Media Ltd, SUMCD 4133
The Celtic Harp Collection, Claire Hamilton, e2 ETD CD/003
Celtic Myths, Claire Hamilton (harp and spoken word), Music Collection
        International ETD CD/157

Websites

Claire Hamilton: www.livingmyths.com
http://vassun.vassar.edu
www.ireland.org
www.irelandnow.com
www.lugodoc.demon.co.uk (for information and amusement)
www.mercyground.com
www.paganism.com
www.sacred-texts.com (Heroic Legends of Ireland)
www.thetain.com

Organisations and Courses

Order of Bards, Ovates and Druids: OBOD, PO Box 1333, Lewes, E. Sussex BN7 3ZG (website: www.druidry.org)

College of Druidism: 4a Minto Street, Edinburgh EH7 4AN

Chrysalis—Awakening the Poet Within: 4 Farlow Road, London SW15 1DT

Pagan Federation: BM Box 5097, London WC1N 3XX

Quest Magazine—Marian Green (books, courses plus magazine): BCM-SCL QUEST, London WC1N 3XX

Hallowquest—Caitlin and John Matthews (courses and newsletter): BCM HALLOWQUEST, London, WC1N 3XX. (website: www.hallowquest.org.uk)

The Source—Sacred Wells and Springs: 29 Rozel Road, Horfield, Bristol BS7 8SQ

Hawkwood College—weekend courses (including some given by Marian Green, Caitlin and John Matthews, Claire Hamilton and Steve Eddy): Painswick Old Road, Stroud, Glos. GL6 7QW

The Wellspring—Sacred Wells & Springs; Jan Shivell, 5 Gladis Place, Llanfoist, Abergavenny, NP7 9NH, Wales